Allison

Vanessa McKay

Allison by Vanessa McKay
Copyright © 2020 by Vanessa McKay

All rights reserved. It is not legal to reproduce, duplicate or transmit any part of this document in either electronic means or printed format. Recording of this publication is strictly prohibited.

For permission requests, contact vmckay@live.com.au

Visit author's website at www.vanessamckay.com

ISBN 978-0-6488713-1-6 (Ebook)
ISBN 978-0-6488713-0-9 (Paperback)

First edition 2020

Published by Tea Time Press

ALLISON

Chapter One

She hated Friday nights. She hated the circle of friends that had sprung up around them. They talked about money, travel, cars, designer houses, and portfolios. It was an effort for Ally to fit in. These were not her people. She hated to see how easily he fitted into their foreign world.

Gavin made his way through the crowd of the Blue Monkey towards her. She could hardly recognise the man she loved. This guy was mostly a jerk. He absently handed her a tall gin and tonic while laughing too loudly at the punch line to Darren's joke. Ally was not so amused.

'Misogynistic arse,' she murmured.

Gavin turned to give her his full attention. 'Sorry, did you say something?'

'Yes, I said that he is a misogynistic arse. Can we go?' She gulped at her drink.

He took hold of her elbow and led her through the double doors to the deserted dining room and spun her around to face him. 'I am so damn sorry, Allison, that my friends offend you, but at least they are trying to have a good time. I appreciate that you least dressed for the occasion, you do look stunning. I just wish you would act as good as you look.' He ran his hands through her hair. 'You have the potential to be so much more than you are, but you reveal nothing. The truth is that you show no personality, nothing. You just do not engage with other people. These are my friends, and they could be your friends too. But you must put some effort into it. Go home if you want to, you can take the car. I will catch a lift.'

'So that is it, you are not coming home then?' Ally stood taller to catch his eyes.

'It's so simple, Ally. I want to stay, but you want to leave. I would like you to stay and enjoy yourself, but if you don't want to stay, that is fine too. Go home. I will see you there.' He released her arm.

'You are really not coming home then?' She searched his face, but his eyes were already elsewhere.

'Ally, please, do not make a scene. We can talk at home. Do you want me to walk you to the car?' His hand was on her shoulder; she felt like a child being scolded and sent to her room for not fitting in.

Allison shrugged out of his hold, crossed her bag strap over her body, and retreated past Gavin's bank teller mates into the chilled June night air of Perth.

It was too late to turn back by the time she realised she had caught the bus into town to meet him and she had no idea where Gavin had parked the car. She waved down a cab, and ten short minutes later she was home. In their bathroom, she undressed while the hot water gushed into their China-blue bath. Ally discarded the dress on the floor, the water soaked her straightened hair back to its natural curls, and with her oatmeal scrub Ally washed the fake off.

When the water had cooled, she dressed in Gavin's striped pyjamas that were an annual Christmas gift from his grandmother he never used. Ally had modified them to suit her. He had once thought it was cute. Sexy, even. She had no idea what he thought of her now.

Outside, the rain traced beads on the windows. Ally sat on the window seat with her journal in hand, pouring her heart out onto the crisp pages, arranging her thoughts so that she could see straight. When she reached a decision she stopped, but the rain kept coming, as the black night sky gave way to the grey sunrise.

Gavin slid out of the taxi, slipping his hand from Deborah's. Ally waited until he had showered and was drying himself to call his name.

'Hey sorry, I didn't mean to wake you.' He crossed the room to kiss her, and she let him. She soaked up the innocence of the act. So many kisses. Lost.

'Late night,' he continued. 'We lost track of time. You didn't wait up for me, did you?'

'Yes, but it is okay. Gavin, we need to talk.'

'Can it wait until I get some sleep,' he said, avoiding her eyes.

'No, Gavin, I need to talk now. Just listen. This won't be hard.' She took a deep breath. 'I could give you a long spiel about it being me and not you. That I just need some space, I need to find myself, but that would be a lie. I don't want to lie to you, Gavin. We have always been truthful with each other, and I want it to stay that way. The truth is, Gavin, you have changed, and I dislike the person you have become.' Ally exhaled. There, it is done, she thought.

'What? Where is this coming from? I am late home one night and you want to leave me? Is that what you are saying? Allison, be reasonable!'

'It is not one night, it is everything, and it is the way that you are now. Your car, your clothes, your books, your goals, your finances, that fucking stereo that I am not supposed to touch that costs four times more than my car.'

'Okay, I will buy you a new car,' said Gavin.

'You are not listening. You never listen to me. I never wanted a blue leather lounge. I am a vegetarian, for fuck's sake. You never consider me; you never ask me what I want. What are my dreams and goals, Gavin? You never ask me about anything anymore. I can't even choose my own clothes or hairstyle. Suddenly you cannot accept me for who I am. You won't let me be who I want to be. You want me to be who you want me to be,' said Ally.

He rubbed the back of his neck. His mouth was dry. 'Ally, we are not kids anymore.'

She watches him move into the kitchen and take two paracetamols from the fruit bowl and wash them down with a coke he pulled from the fridge. 'You need to grow up, Allison,' he said.

'What if I do not intend to grow up the way you want me to, Gavin? What if I like the person I am? What if I am already doing what I want to do?'

'Do you really think singing will ever get you anywhere? Ally, one of us at least has to be realistic; you cannot support a family on a pipe dream.'

ALLISON

'Why not? After Dad left that is all we had, and we managed pretty well. The money that my mum left us, money that she made from singing, is money that we have invested in this house. That is singing money, Gavin, and if my mum can do it, why the hell can't I? I am younger than she was when she started, I don't have multiple sclerosis, and I won't be left high and dry by a bastard of an ex-husband.'

'We can work this out, Ally,' he offered meekly.

'No, Gavin, we are finished. Please do not make this harder than it has to be by trying to pretend we can fix this.'

'So, what happens now?'

'I am going to Renee's. She is looking for a flat mate. You can have everything here. I will come to get my stuff on Monday, and I would appreciate it if you can arrange for me to have what is left of my mum's money. I will send you my account details when I have it sorted. I am sorry, Gavin.'

'Are you really leaving me?'

'Gavin, you must realise that I have to. It was good, it got shit, and now it is done. I will be a singer, a writer, whatever I choose! I am not a banker's wife. I don't want to be paraded out on the weekends. That dress you bought me is not me. It never will be me. Gavin, if that is the kind of girl you want, that girl will never be me,' said Ally.

He considered her for a moment, nodding his head as he conceded that she was no longer the girl that turned him on. When they were younger, her impulsive wildness, her sense of adventure, and her free spirit had captivated and enticed him. He had been under her spell, and he was her hero. Now he was just one of those people that she didn't like. It hurt that she saw him that way, but at the same time he enjoyed being who he was. He enjoyed being with Deborah, and he liked that she had enjoyed him too.

'Ally, I am so sorry,' he said. 'I will always love you. You are my best friend, my family. Understand that I will always be here for you, no matter what.' He held out his arms a final time to hold her. He held her close to his chest and breathed in the sandalwood scent of her hair. A tear fell onto her crown. Once composed, he let his childhood sweetheart, and his first love, go.

Renee opened the door before Ally had the chance to knock, arms open wide ready to console her friend. It surprised her when the call had come. Ally and Gavin had been the 'it' couple back at high school. Everyone thought they would have kids and two dogs by the time they were thirty.

Her composure was gone; Ally sobbed. She let Renee lead her through the house to her new room. It was white-walled, bare, with a new beige carpet. A blank canvas. Furnished only with a bed her friend had quickly made up and a box of tissues. Ally took in sight of her new home with forced optimism but dissolved into tears again.

It was Sunday afternoon before Allison emerged from her room, exhausted but ready to meet her new housemates. She had already met David, Renee's boyfriend, but Scott, who was on a trip around the world and was stopping off to work and raise some much-needed travel capital, was new to her. They exchanged pleasantries over coffee in the garden.

The following day, Renee and Ally smiled gently at each other as they traded places in Nausheen's dimly lit waiting room. Renee thought that a psychic reading that predicted her promising future would go a long way to cheering up her new housemate. Renee's own reading had left her feeling more than a little miffed by the prediction concerning her current relationship, but she hoped that Ally would fare better.

The old woman gestured for Ally to take the seat across from her own.

'Shuffle, please.' Naursheen handed her a deck of tarot cards, soft with use. Ally obeyed.

'Cut them twice with your left hand,' the woman said. 'Are you planning a trip to London? I can see that you are approaching the double green doors of Heathrow Airport with a brown, faux leather backpack, a notebook, and music. There is a man looking away, he is in your past, a finished relationship. There is a second man looking your way. Be wary of this one. Look forward, there is a third man waiting for you. Take care of what you do until he finds you. Find you he will. I am sure of it. Make sure you are available to avoid unnecessary delays to your future happiness. He is very handsome with sandy-brown hair and ocean-green eyes, and he will make you feel that you have come home. This is your true love, the man you will grow old with. This man will help you shed light on the shadows of your past, he will help you see your own true worth, he is the one who will close the door on your demons and open up a window to the future. I don't mean a little toilet window; this is a large bay window coming off a conservatory of delights.' Naursheen giggled.

Patiently Ally waited for her to continue. All she heard was, 'You will meet a man, blah blah blah.' Fortune tellers always say the same thing. Her mum had been a skeptical believer too. She had told Ally that there were truths and wishes in every reading, but not every wish ever came true.

Naursheen ended the silence. 'Your mother says to use the money to travel the world, be free.'

Tears welled in Ally's eyes. 'Is my mum all right there on the other side?'

Naursheen listened.

'She is happy, pain free, and at peace. Music surrounds her. She says to take your warm tweed coat to England.' Naursheen looked over the cards. 'Your mother has told me to say that nothing lasts forever, no matter how awful. What happens at the end is ultimately up to you. You control the things that affect you, the depth of hurt that you cling to. Remember, everything is temporary.'

'Even death?' asked Ally.

'Yes, even death.'

'What is on the other side?'

'The other side? My girl, we are all on the same side. We are all where we should be, and we will all be given the opportunity to do what we were meant to do. Good luck to you, and do not worry. Your future will be wonderful. Take care and go with loving blessings.'

'Well?' Renee stood up as Ally entered the waiting room.

'You are first.' Ally smiled.

'Rubbish. Apparently, if I marry David, we should never have children because it won't last. She said we will only last as long as we have been. I ask you, what does that even mean? The woman talks in riddles. Gran came all the way from the other side of crap knows where to tell me she doesn't like my new haircut, and my butt is too big for leggings! Honestly, can you believe the gall?'

ALLISON

'Renee, I am surprised at you being outraged by a bit of make believe. She was vague with me too. Like you said, the woman talks in riddles and makes no bloody sense.'

Chapter Two

It took three months for David to organise the housewarming party he had promised Ally during her first week in the house. Together, David and Scott took care of most of the arrangements.

To celebrate Ally's arrival, the boys arranged everything from invites to ice. Ignoring Ally's protests, they set up a spit-roasted lamb outside, and every basin and sink throughout the house was filled with ice, cans, and stubbies. Their saving grace had been the karaoke machine. It was Ally's first party without Gavin, and she was having a hard time adjusting to being alone. Socialising was hard. Never one to intrude, Ally was finding it difficult striking up a conversation with new people. She took to her room from time to time to breathe in the darkness, cool her brow, and strengthen her resolve.

The growing crowd of twenty-somethings found their niches with apparent social ease. Some were playing spin the bottle like children on the lounge room floor, others were dancing on the lawn or deep in conversation and general piss-taking. Six blokes with dyed hair were trying their luck at the dartboard, which was hanging precariously from a piece of electrical wire off the back fence.

On her way to the bathroom, Ally found Renee sitting on the edge of her bed crying. 'Are you okay? What has David done now?' Ally smiled sympathetically as she sat beside Renee and wrapped an arm around her shoulder.

'I am okay, Ally, it is just. LOOK!' Renee handed her a white stick stained with two blue lines.

'Is that what I think it is?'

'Ally, haven't you ever taken a pregnancy test before? I am pregnant! Fuck! Fuck! Shit! Cunt! Naursheen told me not to get too involved, not to have children with 'this one'. Fuck! Shit! Fuck!'

'Oh, Renee, could the test be wrong? Naursheen could be wrong, and thankfully though, bear in mind that I will deny ever saying it if those two lines become my god child we have options. It is not the middle ages. Ask yourself if David is the one, the man you want to raise a family with. Fuck what Naursheen said, this is your life.'

'Oh, Ally, it is so easy for you, look at you. You are beautiful, smart, funny, exciting, and creative. Now look at me. What am I? Always the tallest girl in my class and by high school the fattest arsed too. I was a giant. A spotty, scraggy-haired, unattractive giant. Great for goal keeping but not to take on a date. You don't appreciate what it is like to have your heart broken time and time again.'

'Oh my god! You are so wrong, Renee. You are so exquisite, always the life of the party, my beacon of light and laughter. You are the most genuine, caring, loving person I have ever met. Please don't think so little of yourself, and don't you dare sell your dreams short. You have always been my role model.'

'Huh?'

'Don't scoff at me, young lady, just admit that every word is true.'

'David is the first man who ever made me feel like a real woman. When he touches me, I don't have to pretend that he is doing it right, because he is. He gave me my first orgasm. Ally, can you imagine? I have faked it so many times, with some many duds, I was afraid of letting out the secret.'

'What secret?'

'You know, how we all fake it to please our man. Oh god, I bet you never had to.'

'What? No, I never had to. Have I? This may sound dumb, but I am not sure. Gavin is my first, my only one, so how would I recognise that what I was feeling was an orgasm? Gavin would tell me I was having one, but thinking back, what do I know?'

'My god, Ally, have you never given yourself one?'

'What? No! Never mind me, what are you going to do?'

Renee wiped her eyes dry. 'Nothing. I may tell David after the party, or not. I need to think this through. Tonight, is not about this. Tonight, is about celebrating my best friend's new life. Come on, Ally, sing me some Pink!'

Under the coloured lights from the karaoke machine, Renee and Ally picked their four favourite Pink songs. The machine switched from playing on auto to the introduction of the first

ALLISON

song. Renee raised the volume and left Ally on the stage. Ally's voice filled the air.

'This used to be a …' The energy from the vocals surged through Ally's body, giving her the strength she needed to face the audience. She was home. The group were mostly strangers to Ally. They cheered and applauded as she went through the songs on her playlist.

'Another! Another!' the crowd cheered. Renee and David cheered loudest.

Scott chose 'Kai Sahn' by Cold Chisel, handed her a drink, and gestured for her to continue. The crowd shouted for more, and she had no option but to please them. It took hours to exhaust the ongoing playlist and satiate the crowd of new friends, singing along, dancing, and applauding.

She loved the sound of applause. Her mum had called it the rhythmic drum of appreciation. Bliss. It had been some time since Ally had had such a captive audience. None of these people had ever heard Ally sing before. Most did not have any idea who she was. There was a buzz of curiosity in the crowd. Renee and David cheered front and centre, leading chants of 'Sing us another.' The chants echoed through the quiet streets of Manning. Tonight, Ally was an entertainer, she was everything that she wanted to be. For the first time without her mum by her side, Ally was holding the crowd on her own.

Scott appeared next to the karaoke machine and chose the next song. 'Chains.' Ally sang the song, then another and another, until it was one in the morning. Finally, the rock songs gave way to softer ballads, songs of broken hearts. She sang Lionel Richie's 'Hello'. She made it her song: once it had been hers and Gavin's, but tonight, she owned the poetry in her music.

Scott watched Ally from the edge of the crowd. Only leaving his spot to replenish her gin and tonic. He couldn't keep his eyes off her. A few times throughout the night he caught her eye, and they exchanged smiles. When she thanked him for the drinks, her full lips framed her smile, her green eyes sparkled. He watched her every move, when she licked her lips and when her hips rolled with the music. He surveyed every curve of her body. He wanted to touch her, feel her. He wanted her to see him too.

Exhausted, she said farewell to the thinning crowd. Scott walked up to the makeshift stage and held out his hand, urging her to take it. Despite his dark hair and chiseled features, he lacked the character she liked in men. But his broad, suntanned frame was so different to Gavin's pale, slim build. She liked that Scott was meaty; she did not want to be reminded of Gavin tonight.

'Dance with me, Ally, I have been watching you all night. Let me hold you close.'

'Watching me all night you say, interesting.' She smiled.

'I could be your biggest fan.'

'My only fan.' She laughed.

'How can you say that? You single-handedly entertained the crowd all night. This party will be the talk of parties for years to come. Because of you. Because you are...amazing.'

'Thanks, Scott.' She blushed. 'It is just hard to hear, but it is what I want to hear. I want my music to be taken seriously. My mum made a living from singing. She was amazing, and she said that I was better than her. I don't agree with that, she was incredible; her pitch and range were something else. I will have to work hard to be as good as her, but I am willing to do that work.'

ALLISON

Scott wrapped one hand around her waist and the other held her palm to his chest. Ally relaxed into his embrace, and the two swayed in time to the music.

As the night wore on, the tired crowd thanked their hosts, congratulated Ally on her talent, and made their way home. David and Renee were the last to say goodnight.

In the chill of the early Perth morning, Ally and Scott slow danced into the sunrise, holding onto each other like lovers, feeding off the warmth of the other's bodies. She inhaled his scent and was lured into the hard, protective blanket his body had become. His arms supported her and pulled her tight into his body. Ally's head rested in the space between his neck and shoulder. His chin rested gently on her head. Both were tired, but neither wanted to let go.

After separating from Gavin, Ally had missed the feeling of being protected most, of being loved and safe. Until now. She began to pull away.

She did not want to get attached to Scott. He was leaving soon to photograph the world. She couldn't let herself.

'I am sorry, but I have to go to bed.' She yawned. 'I will see you in the morning. It was a great party. Thank you for organising it.'

'Yes, it was, and you were awesome. Do you want a coffee?' he offered.

'No, thank you. I really need to get some sleep.'

'No thank you kiss?'

She stepped towards him and kissed his shadowed cheek then moved quickly out of reach before he could take it further. He stood alone, surrounded by party litter. Desire coursing through his body, Scott felt the warmth of the morning sun on his back, felt the memory of the warmth of her body. 'Ally,' he whispered to the dawn.

Ally flopped onto her bed amidst the bountiful cushions. She smiled as she lay back, breathing in the scented cushions that she collected the day before from Fremantle market. Gavin would hate everything in her room. Ally loved this part of her newfound independence. She finally felt in charge of her own life: every choice she made was hers. From the food she ate to the clothes she wore.

She reluctantly stood up to undress for bed when there was a light rapping on her door. Ally opened the door to Scott.

'Oh, I thought you were Renee,' said Ally, embarrassed at being caught in her underwear.

'Well, that's an interesting thought! Does David know what you two girls get up to?' Scott flashed her a lopsided smile.

'Don't be crass, it is nothing like that, I just thought she might like to talk.' Ally reached for her bathrobe as Scott walked into her room and held out a gin and tonic. She took it reluctantly—she wanted to sleep, but she also wanted him out of her room. Ally suggested that they go to the lounge room, excusing the non-existent mess in her room.

Scott followed her through and sat next to her on the couch.

'Great party, the best that we have had by far,' he said.

'I really enjoyed it. What a great crowd,' she said.

'Yeah, I noticed you enjoy being the centre of attention. You surprised me tonight, Ally, I saw another side of you up there on the stage. I would never have thought that you were such a show-off.'

'Show-off?' Ally laughed, hoping that he was teasing.

'Yeah, show-off. Did it bother Gavin? Was that why he left you? Renee said he was quiet and reserved. I guess he was the dignified type.'

Ally took a large swig of her drink, concerned at where this conversation was heading. Was he judging her? No, surely not. He was usually so nice. Maybe she was just being paranoid. She had been drinking loads, then she had what she thought was an unsuccessful turn at a party bong, and now the sun was up, and she was having another drink.

'I think I have had enough to drink. I should go to bed.' She put the glass on the table as he reached out to hold her arm. 'I didn't mean to offend you. My last girlfriend was an exotic dancer, and wherever we went, she was always finding an excuse to show off her body. She was always getting me into fights with other men. Sorry, I didn't mean to compare you two. Please stay and finish your drink with me.' Scott passed her the glass.

'Okay, just this one and I am off to bed.'

'Yes, me too.'

He listened to her breathing heavily for a while. 'Ally, are you asleep?' Gently he rocked her by the shoulders. Certain that she was out, he lifted her up and carried her to her bedroom. He laid her on her bed, untied her robe, and pulled the sides apart. The soft, white flesh of her torso exposed; he kissed a line across her body.

Clumsily he removed her bra. She moaned softly as he took one hard nipple into his mouth, sucking it between his teeth, teasing the other with his thumb and forefinger. Then he bit down hard. He stood above her and noticed gooseflesh on her arms and chest.

'You won't be cold much longer, dear,' he whispered. 'Time for my private viewing, Allison.' He slid her panties down her legs and left them dangling from one ankle. As he rubbed one hand along the length of her, he used the other to slide his own pants down. He relished her readiness.

She had had too much to drink. She remembered a party. Through her fog, he fucked her hard. His cock pulsated deep into her. When he was done, he lingered until his cock went limp. There were several flashes in the darkness before Ally was alone and could rest in the memory of Gavin.

When Ally woke early that afternoon, she found herself naked under the covers, she smelt the undeniable odour of sex on the sheets. She still dreamt of Gavin, and last night had felt so real. It must have been a dream, she couldn't remember how she got to bed, but she was sure that she was alone.

Chapter Three

Ally turned to Renee at the door to the Victoria Park Women's Clinic. 'Are you one hundred percent sure that you want to go through with this? I am here for you whatever you decide, but once this is done, there is no going back.'

'I know. I get that you may not understand, but I have to get my life together. I don't know whether I want to marry David. I honestly don't think I want to spend the rest of my life with him. For crying out loud, he is a party boy, not a father. A baby would tie me to David for the rest of my life. I know that right now David is good for me. I feel wanted, loved, and sexy, and that is how I want to feel for now. A baby would take that away. Please don't hate me for this, Ally. I know that I'm being selfish. I just can't be a mother right now.'

Ally smiled sympathetically and nodded. She linked arms with Renee and led her inside the stone building. Lime-green, vinyl chairs lined the surgery walls, mostly taken up with women and their accompanying partners, sisters, or friends. Two teenage girls no older than sixteen sat in one corner, a woman and her partner in another. Other patients dotted the middle rows, distracted women staring into outdated magazines. Ally smiled self-consciously, picked up a magazine, and sat while Renee approached the desk to register.

It was a long, almost silent, wait. The rustle of magazine pages being turned, and the tick of the clock were the only sounds in the tiny room. No one spoke out loud, they breathed words in whispers about everyday mundane things to the people they had come in with. Women disappeared through the 'staff only' door as gowned staff called their names. When it was Renee's turn to go, Ally kissed her on the cheek, hugged her tightly, and told her she would return to collect her in the afternoon as arranged.

'Thank you,' Renee whispered.

At home Ally busied herself with cleaning the breakfast mess away. They were a fun group of people to share a home with, but none of them liked housework. Ally was at home throughout the day, as she worked a few nights a week running the karaoke show at the Underground. It seemed like she did most of the housework, which wasn't ideal, but today it gave her something else to focus on.

David had set up a large pin-up board over the sink to document pictures of the 'fun times' they shared in the house. Photos from their first house party a few weeks ago were plastered in the left-hand corner. There was a photo of her dancing with Scott, and it occurred to her that they had hardly crossed paths since that night. He must have understood that she was not ready for a relationship; she needed time, and he was leaving soon. Since

ALLISON

the party he had been on a week-long tour of Margaret River and had taken extra hours to save for his trip around the world. It was a relief to her that he was focused on his goals and doing what it took to achieve them. She thought that if she were braver and more assured, she would consider doing the same. 'Imagine me, a global, jet-setting singer. A woman of the world,' she said to no one as she shook the suds off her hands.

Ally was now pacing the floor. It was three o'clock, but there was still no word from the clinic. David would be home from work soon. He had been told that the girls were spending the day shopping in town. Panicking, she grabbed her bag and car keys and was on her way out of the door when the phone rang.

'Good afternoon, can I speak to Allison Jones please?'

'Yes, this is she.'

'My name is Maria. I am calling from Vic Park Surgery.'

'Is everything okay?' Ally interrupted.

'No, I am sorry to say that there was a small complication during your friend's procedure, and we transported her to King Edward Memorial Hospital in Subiaco. We have been informed that she is in a stable condition, but chances are they will keep her there for a few days to be sure.'

'Can I see her?' Ally asked when she caught her breath.

'Yes, and perhaps you can take her some personal items you know, nightwear, toiletries, and so on,' suggested the voice on the phone.

'Yes, thank you I will.' She hung up the phone, her head was spinning. Ally's thoughts raced... *What was she going to do now? She would have to tell David, wouldn't she? Oh God, but she promised Renee she wouldn't ever, ever say a word. Shit!*

Hurriedly she packed a bag for Renee. The door slammed shut behind her as she left the house.

Renee was the colour of concrete. Ally took her hand and whispered her name. 'What happened? Are you awake?'

Renee opened her eyes and smiled at Ally.

'I started hemorrhaging, so they had to give me a full anesthetic, and it took some time to stop the bleeding. I needed a blood transfusion.' Renee shrugged. 'That is all I know.'

'But will you be okay?'

'Yes, I will. Don't worry. I'm just tired and crampy. Ally, you didn't tell David, did you?'

'No, he was still at work when I got the call from the clinic, so he probably thinks we are still out shopping. I will have to tell him something when I go home without you. What do you want me to say?'

'I don't know, but if I can get out of here, we won't have to say anything.'

'I am not sure that is such a good idea. You look awful. The nurse said you would be here for two days. Renee, you don't need me to tell you this is very serious. You are a nurse!'

'So, I know how to look after myself,' she said as tears streamed down her cheeks. 'No lectures, please, Ally.'

Ally held her friend close as tears and snot flowed onto her shoulder. The shuddering, ugly crying of her dearest friend's pain opened her own flood gates, and for a time the two women cried together until they were both spent.

'What are we going to tell David?' asked Ally.

'We will tell him I had a turn. You brought me to the hospital, and they said I had to rest for a while. They ran some tests, and it turns out that I have a virus, and I need bed rest,' said Renee.

'Okay, sounds good. I can look after you during the day and make sure you rest up!'

'Better load up some movies and junk food, I feel the blues coming on. Help me get out of here, Ally.'

Chapter Four

'Hey, David, check out the vision that just entered the room.'

Scott was smiling as he leered at Ally. She ignored him and asked David where Renee was.

'She is still getting ready.' David shrugged and sighed. 'Ally, is everything all right? It is just that she has had this virus for weeks now. I am starting to think it is more than being off colour.'

'What I think David means is that he is not getting any, Ally,' said Scott.

'Scott, this is serious,' David said.

Ally felt sorry for him. It wasn't fair that he didn't know. 'I know. Don't worry, David. I am sure life will return to normal soon. Meanwhile, I will see what is taking her so long. She probably can't decide which of her hundred and one pair of shoes goes best with her fabulous outfit.'

'Speaking of fabulous, you look quite the dish yourself.' Scott eyed her up and down shamelessly. 'You will sing tonight.' It was a statement, not a question.

'I rarely go out with a plan to sing at other people's parties, but if the opportunity arises, I might. Why not? It is hard to say no when you are asked.' Ally smiled as she spun on a heel and left the room.

David punched Scott in the arm. 'You like Ally. I think there is something going on between you two. I hear the pitter patter of horny feet and squeaking doors some nights. I know you two have done the deed.'

'Yes, but don't make a big deal of it. Say nothing to Renee either, you know what girls are like. I don't want this fling to turn into a relationship. She is a little too out there for me. The singing and showing off are just one thing. What's up with the herbs, the aromatherapy, yoga, and crystals? Plus, she goes to those charlatan fortune tellers. I think she has a running appointment with one. Can you imagine me with someone like that?'

David raised his brows, unsure of what to say. Ally and Scott had only slept together once, the night Renee came home from hospital. Ally had not been able to sleep and was in the lounge room journalling when Scott had returned home late. The two had talked and shared a bottle of wine. One thing led to another, and before she understood what was happening, she was enticed into his bedroom. The combination of his good looks, the loneliness she felt that night, and the weight of her friend's heavy secret had made her vulnerable. Ally had not told Renee about Scott, and as far as she knew he had not told David. It hadn't felt right. He didn't feel right or maybe she didn't want him to feel right because he was going away, or because she was still recovering from her wounds, from her severed connection with Gavin. Scott had looked at her with his dark brown eyes and made her feel wanted, but it had just been sex, and she was determined to keep her distance rather than risk her heart in a relationship with him.

'Renee, I hope you are decent. I am coming in.' Ally slowly opened the bedroom door.

'Yes, please come in, Ally,' Renee called from her ensuite, her voice gravelly.

'Are you all right, Renee? What's wrong?'

'Oh, Ally, I was getting ready, and I know this makes little sense, but I started thinking about the baby. What would it be like, to be a mum. How it would change my life. I wouldn't be going out tonight to an air force cocktail party. I would be busy being a mum. I like the thought of being a mum. I'm not just a happy party girl without a care in the world. The problem is, Ally, I do care, I do.'

Ally held her friend in a tight embrace.

'Oh god, David will wonder what is going on, we better move on before he starts off with his lesbian love scene imaginations.' Renee tapped Ally on the shoulder and pulled away.

'Goodness, Renee, look at the state of you. You don't have a chance of getting it on with me looking like that. You look positively ridiculous, all panda eyed and snotty. But that dress and shoes are fabulous. You show promise.'

Later at the party, Renee took Ally by the hand. 'Come on, I want you to meet someone,' she said stealing her away from a group of men discussing the latest football results. Ally was grateful for the intervention.

ALLISON

'Ally, this is Robert. Robert is originally from Sydney and is currently based in Bullsbrook. Robert, this is my best friend, Ally. She is a singer, and as you can see for yourself, a stunner.'

Renee swiftly left the pair to return to David and the group discussing the grossest thing they had ever seen their pets do. As she joined them, the group was laughing at Harry's German shepherd who was a master at licking his own arse and eating his own shit.

'Well, subtlety was never one of Renee's virtues, but it is nice to meet you, Robert.'

'It is very nice to meet you too. Sorry if you feel you are being ambushed. I was talking to Renee at the bar, and I asked her to introduce us. I saw you sing at the house. Unfortunately, I had to leave to take my date home. She claimed to have had an allergic reaction to David's punch.'

'Oh, was she alright?' Ally did her best to hide her disappointment.

'I don't know. I think so. It was just a date, my sister set me up with her. I don't think she enjoyed herself with me any more than I did with her. That is a terrible thing to say. I sound awful.'

'No, not at all, I understand.' Ally smiled at him.

'Can I get you a drink?' he offered.

'Yes, please, a gin and tonic would be lovely.' She smiled broadly.

'I will be right back.' Robert turned and disappeared into the crowd of people.

Scott walked up behind Ally and swiftly ran his hand up her leg towards the hem of her dress. Ally slapped his hand away. 'What are you doing?' Ally looked annoyed.

He laughed. 'Allison, you know you will want me up there later. You will let me have my way with you. But... until you see sense, I am going to play with that blonde over there. Perfect body and dumb as shit. The type of girl you expect to find at these things.'

Ally watched him make his way to the blonde; without warning he grabbed her breasts from behind, and when she spun around to see who it was, he pushed her into the water.

'I would have thought it a little early for that.' Robert handed her a gin and tonic. 'That kind of thing usually happens a little closer to the end of the night.'

'He is just a jerk. What kind of man does that?' Ally said shaking her head. 'The poor girl.'

The poor girl, however, had her arm around Scott's neck and was laughing. Scott had jumped into the pool and was re-moving her knickers, which he then spun over his head like a lasso. Having had his fun, he left her alone in the pool and went into the house in search of dry clothes. The show was over, and the onlookers returned to their conversations.

The girl had stopped laughing now that no one was watching.

'Are you okay? He has ruined your beautiful dress.' Ally offered her a hand to get out of the pool.

'Just let it go; we used to date. He has a habit of luring me into a scene only to embarrass me and dump me again. Now he is angry at me. I don't know why I keep falling for it. He must be right about me.'

'Right about what?' Ally asked.

'That I deserve it because I am just, you know, a dumb blonde.' She let Ally help her out of the pool and followed Scott into the house.

ALLISON

Robert joined Ally by the pool. 'You share a house with him, don't you? What is he like to live with? If he gives you any trouble, let me know. I would like the opportunity to sort him out for you. I don't mean to sound so macho, it is just, that is not the way you treat a girl. I was taught to respect people.'

'I have never seen him like that before, it was strange.'

'I have heard he has a reputation, Ally, be careful. I would hate to see you get hurt.'

'No fear there, thank you, Robert. Do you want to get out of here and go for a walk?'

Renee watched her two friends leave the party. She smiled to herself and hoped that they had found a connection. She had known Robert through their mutual circle of friends for a year and thought he would be perfect for Ally. She could sense something was brewing in the house between Scott and Ally, and she knew Scott's type too well to let that go any further. She had seen the games he played with the women in his life. Scott was only up for a good time and that was it. Ally deserved better and needed more than that. Robert was the answer. Renee was sure of it.

As they left the noise of the party behind them, the two new friends talked and laughed about the antics of their shared acquaintances. Ally took in the rounded features of his face, friendly and warm, like his character. He was taller than her, with broad shoulders. His sandy hair was combed back from his forehead, and his sexy, green eyes watched her as she spoke. He hung onto her every word. Ally listened intently as he spoke about his work in the air force. She pictured him in his navy-blue uniform. Robert was a trained pilot and spoke of the fierce competition to achieve rank and a plane.

They walked along Mends Street to the Swan River, stopping at the Atomic Espresso for a drink. When it closed, they walked hand in hand along the river back to the party, relaxed in each other's company.

Stopping at the gate, Ally could hear Scott and David yelling their Aussie! Aussie! Aussie! chant to the roar of the drunken crowd. Robert leaned close to her, brushing his lips past hers in a soft and tender kiss. She wanted more but continued gently, afraid of breaking the spell. They explored each other's lips. The kiss reminded Ally of the softness of rose petals, and she revelled in the feeling of being cherished.

Robert felt something unknown to him, something that he didn't recognise. It couldn't be love, but if he was to fall in love, he knew at that moment that it was Ally he wanted to fall in love with.

Scott burst through the gate, breaking their spell. 'Where have you been?'

'We were just walking, I...why am I explaining myself?' Ally said.

'We have to go! I will bring the car around; if you are done, perhaps you could help your friend Renee with that sloth of hers?' Scott pushed between the pair.

'I can help you,' said Robert and led Ally back to the party.

At home, Scott, Ally and Renee unloaded David from the car and carried him to his bed. Renee got him a bucket, a towel, and a packet of paracetamol. She thanked Scott and Ally for their help and bid them both goodnights.

Scott turned to Ally. 'Why did you go outside with the flyboy?'

ALLISON

'You mean Robert?'

He shrugged. 'I guess—if that's his name.'

'If you must know, I grew tired of the party, so we took a walk to talk and get some fresh air. What do you care? You were busy all night with the blonde. What I do is none of your business anyway! I do not have to explain myself to you.'

'Oh, okay, I get it now. You were acting out. I see you are jealous. I don't like jealous Allison, it is very unbecoming. We have a thing going on here, but it is just a thing, you know. It does not tie me to you. I do not expect any girl I take to a party to have it off with some joker in the car park. That was rude, Allison, I am very disappointed.'

He was standing too close to Ally. Her back was up against the kitchen bench, his face an inch from hers. His voice was low, but his face contorted into someone she didn't recognise.

'I was not having it off with anyone. Robert and I were just getting to know each other. You came out as we were coming back in. And I don't recall that I went to that party as your girl, as you so easily claim. I went to that party at the invitation of Renee. Now, if you'll excuse me, I am going to bed.' She tried to push past him.

'Correction, Allison. We are going to bed.' He took her hand, rolled her wrist behind her back, and walked her down the opposite hall to his bedroom. Closing the door behind them, he threw her down on the bed.

When she tried to get up, he hit her hard across the face. She saw stars. He pinned her shoulder to the bed with one hand while his free hand worked a sock into her mouth, then he muffled her screams with tape. Pinning her firmly to the bed with his knees, he tied her arms above her head, between the bannisters of the headboard.

'You fucken bitches are all alike. I know you fucked him. I bet you let him bend you over the bins and fuck you there like the trash that you are. I will fuck him right out of you. No one will touch you once I am finished with you.'

Ally shook her head, pleading, trying to make him understand that she wanted him to stop! She tried to use her legs and hips to push him off, he saw fighting as a sign she wanted him. He tore the cotton dress from her trembling body and then ripped off her panties. In one move he pierced her with his cock, thrusting deep and hard. Whispering hateful words in her ears, he came, wild-eyed.

Rape didn't satisfy Scott Clarke. He put a pillow over her face and beat it with his fists. No one could hear her screams. She could hear her blood pumping, her breath. The last thing she heard was the clicking of camera shutters until she couldn't hold on any longer and the world turned black.

Ally woke in the harsh morning light. Afraid and in pain, she struggled against the ties holding her on Scott Clarke's bed. The room and mattress were stripped bare. All signs of him were gone.

'Help!' she yelled. Still gagged, her call for help was muffled and came out in a primal squeal. Her next shout broke through, stopping the sounds of Renee and David moving around the kitchen.

David appeared at the door. Confused, he was unsure of what to make of the scene before him. Polaroid pictures of Ally, taken while she was unconscious were scattered around on the floor of the room.

'God. It is okay, Ally, he's gone.' David set about untying her. 'Renee! Get in here!'

Renee ran into the room.

David left, mumbling. 'I will call the police. We must get this bastard; I want to kill him! Kill him!'

As Renee went with Ally to the hospital, the search for Scott Clarke was launched. All routes out of Perth were being watched. The police alerted checkpoints at the state exits. Soon Scott Clarke would be all over crime stoppers; he was about to become one of Western Australia's most wanted men.

Chapter Five

Ally couldn't face returning to that house. After a week recovering in hospital, a barrage of medical tests and police questioning, she took up Gavin's offer to stay with him until she was on her feet again.

'Okay, Ally, you know where everything is. Nothing has changed since you were last here. Nothing except your absence.' Gavin smiled and touched her arm softly.

She smiled back at him. 'Thanks for letting me stay here. I just couldn't go back to the house. Even with the locks changed I wouldn't feel safe. I feel awful for Renee and David; it can't be nice for them either. I promise that I won't be in your hair for long.' Ally exhaled. 'I feel better just being away from there. It is nice being here with you. It feels safe. Thank you, Gavin.'

'Stay here as long as you need to. I know we weren't working as lovers, but I had hoped that when our emotions were not so raw, we could be friends. Always. I will always be here for you, Ally. I am not saying that to ease my own conscience for not having lived up to my part of the relationship but because I will always love you. I will always be here for you, no matter what. I promise.' He wrapped his arms tightly around Ally's soft frame.

She winced from the residual pain of her bruises but returned the embrace with the same intensity. It was not a passionate embrace; it was a comforting, familiar hold, a relic left over from their former relationship. Friendship, in its simplest, most honest forms.

'I have moved into the spare room so you can have the master bedroom.' He pulled away to see her face.

'No, Gavin,' she said. 'I don't want the master bedroom. I have had enough of that leather bedhead and leopard print doona. You keep it. I will be happy in the spare room.'

'You really don't like leather and leopard?' he asked.

'No,' she said, smiling.

'So that was not a great Christmas present for you?'

'No, not your best work.'

'Why didn't you tell me?' he asked.

'I did Gavin, I told you a thousand times, but you kept telling me it's fashion baby.' She threw her hands up in the air.

'Oops, sorry, Ally. I realise now that I could be insensitive,' he said, looking at the ground.

'It's okay, Gavin. I really didn't mind you expressing yourself.'

'Okay, well, express yourself in the spare room any way you want to.' He smiled sheepishly.

'Thank you, but I won't be staying here that long. I can't. It wouldn't be fair to you or me. We can't move on with the rest of our lives when we are living underfoot. I love you and appreciate what you are doing for me now, but this is not a long-term arrangement. Okay?'

'Ally, I don't have to remind you that you have been through an horrific ordeal. You need a safe place to recuperate. I want this to be that space. I want to give you that space and be here for you, for as long as you need it.'

'I love you for that. Please give me a hand to get my stuff out of the car.'

'No, put the kettle on, I will bring in the rest of your things,' he said, picking up her keys from the hall table.

After dinner, they sat side by side on the couch watching Dr Who reruns and sharing a plate of Camembert cheese, quince, and crackers with a bottle of Rose.

'Just like the old days.' Gavin smiled. He had missed Ally, and while he agreed that they could not return to a relationship again, she was still his best friend. She needed him, and he wanted to be there for her. He knew she had no one else to look after her. After what that bastard had done to her, she needed a haven to recover in, and he intended to see that it was with him.

Sitting side by side on the couch seemed familiar and safe to Ally. She had once loved Gavin to a fault. She had lost herself in him, tried to be what he wanted her to be, and failed. She planned to look for somewhere else to live soon. This new arrangement, while generous of Gavin, did not feel fair to him. He didn't owe her anything. It wasn't right for her to depend on him. The sooner she found her feet the better, but for now, it felt nice to be here, close to him, safe.

Chapter Six

'Good morning, sleepyhead,' said Gavin, flipping a pancake with practised precision.

'Good morning to you too.' She yawned.

'Did you get much sleep last night? I have made you some pancakes.'

'I feel myself drifting off to sleep and then bang, I am awake. It is hard to stop... pancakes smell good, I hoped that was what I was smelling. They look delicious. And berries too!'

'Take a seat, madam, and I shall fetch you a plate.'

When Gavin set a plate of hot fluffy pancakes in front of Ally, she smiled. 'Just like mum used to make. Thank you, but you should not have gone to all this trouble.'

'No trouble, Ally, it is worth the all the effort to see you smile.'

He placed a plate of sliced bananas and strawberries on the table next to a jug of maple syrup.

'I love bananas, this looks so yummy! Thank you, Gavin.'

'You have been cooped up inside for weeks, so I was wondering if you would like to take a walk into Freo today? We could go to the markets then maybe we can grab some fish and chips for lunch. Cicerellos on the foreshore?' He sat across from her, watching her, one eyebrow raised in anticipation of her reply.

'Gavin.' She put down her knife and fork. 'You don't have to wait on me. I know you hate the markets, but I appreciate the sentiment,' she said, smiling.

'Ally!' He swallowed her name down with a mouthful of pancake and syrup. 'I do not hate the markets. The truth is, I have missed hanging out with you, and I would love to do something with you today. Ally, you have been through such a horrible time. I just want you to feel good again.'

'I have to admit that it would be nice to get out of the house,' she said.

'Yes, it would, so eat up and get dressed.' He smiled.

The Sunday crowd flowed around them, pushing Ally and Gavin along from one jammed stall to the next. The air was thick with the smell of fish, incense, oils, and candle wax. They loitered in the music shop. Ally found a Kasey Chambers album for eight dollars and promised not to play it when Gavin was home.

'You just aren't cultured enough,' she retorted countering his sneers at her choice.

'You are not putting that nasal noise in my stereo,' he warned, waggling his finger.

She bit the finger to quiet his noise. The pair bantered their way around the nooks and crannies of Fremantle Markets. He allowed her to assault his sense of smell at the essential oil shop and waited with practised patience when she bought bottles of lavender, geranium, and sandalwood for her nerves and peppermint to help lift her mood.

He laughed at what he always thought was her gullibility, and, as she had always done, before she accepted his good humoured taunts graciously.

Thirsty, they headed to the bar for a cold beer and watched the didgeridoo buskers across the market lane. After a short visit to the joke and magic stall, the pair made their way out of the markets through the fruit sellers, stopping to collect a tray of skewered chocolate covered strawberries before exiting the markets, weaving their way through Fremantle lane ways and side streets to the foreshore.

Ally took off her shoes to walk barefoot on the green. She held Gavin's hand because it was the natural thing to do.

'Ally?'

Looking up, she saw him. Handsome, sandy features and vivid, ocean-green eyes. 'Robert? Wow, it's nice to run into you, I haven't seen you since...' Her voice trailed off. She didn't know how to finish.

'Yes, I know, that party.' Robert was looking at Gavin, shifting his gaze to their hands as he spoke.

'Oh, I am sorry. This is Gavin. Gavin, Robert.' She let go of Gavin's hand.

'Pleased to meet you.' Gavin held out his hand. Robert took it and gave it a firm handshake.

'You too. Sorry, but I have to go. I am already late. I am meeting up with some friends. It was nice seeing you, Ally.' He walked through the pair in the opposite direction.

Gavin watched her watch Robert walk away. 'He likes you. He seems nice. Do you like him?' Gavin nudged her.

'Yes, we went for a walk once at a party. He kissed me, and then I never heard from him again. Until now. And he took off pretty damn fast.' She sighed.

'You do realise that he saw us holding hands and he probably thinks we are together. If you are interested in him Ally perhaps you need to explain to the poor bloke.'

'What am I supposed to say? It is okay, this is my ex-boyfriend. I have moved back in with him because my flat mate raped me and left me for dead. Sorry I didn't call. Huh? He doesn't need my shit any more than you do. He is a really nice bloke; he just doesn't need my shit.'

Gavin moved his arm around her shoulder. 'Don't underestimate a man who has feelings for you. I recognise the look he gave you.'

Sitting at a table on the jetty outside of Cicerellos, Ally and Gavin ate fish and chips with potato scallops smothered in salt and vinegar. They watched in companionable silence as the sun set over Fremantle harbour.

Chapter Seven

Deborah dumped a clump of files on Gavin's desk.

'I just do not understand why she has to stay with you.' She planted her backside on his desk and bent forward to look him in the eye.

'Do we have to talk about this again?' Gavin returned her stare.

'No, not here, anyway. How about I come over tonight and we can discuss it then?'

'Yes, sure, why not? Ally will be at her karate class until nine, so I will make dinner and show you that nothing has changed between us.'

'Just so you know, as long as that girl is under your roof, things have changed. Now in the meantime, I want you to review these archives for anomalies.' She tapped the top of the files with her pen.

'What? Is that even a thing?'

'Gavin, it is a thing because I say it is. Do not mess around with this. You are due back out the front at twelve o'clock for the lunchtime shift. I want these done before then. Please.'

'Yes, ma'am, I will get this done,' he said, saluting her.

'Don't be an arse, Gavin.' She tousled his hair playfully. He pushed her hand away and turned his attention to the files, mouthing her last words like a child.

Stepping outside of the dojo, Ally and Renee squeal with delight, their new yellow belts around their waist.

'I can't believe we passed,' Renee said.

'I know, but with all the work we put in, we would be a pair of sad sacks if we failed. Just think, we could be black belts one day. Woo hoo!' Ally punched the air.

'Those extra classes we took really paid off, Ally. I am so glad that you talked me into coming along with you.'

'Thank you for coming with me. I am not sure that I would have been brave enough to do it myself. Learning the self-defense components has been really confronting. Some of the partner work was a little too realistic.'

'But you did it, Ally, you learned how to turn yourself from victim to victor. You could have done this on your own. Ally, you can do anything. Plus, Sensei Dan is awesome and more than a little dreamy to boot.'

'For an older guy he is hot, but we didn't know that the days we sat out in the carpark daring one another to go inside. I am so glad that we did it. Sensei Dan is helping me to become strong again, up here.' Ally tapped her temples.

'Seems so silly to think that we parked here for three nights in a row watching people going inside before we got fed up with

ALLISON

ourselves and braved going in!' Renee laughed. 'It is a whole new world for us, Ally, and they have initiated us into the ranks of karate warrior! Shall we get a drink to celebrate?'

'I can't. Deborah is coming over and Gavin wants us to meet again, be friends, to make things easier for him. Apparently, she has been giving him a hard time at work, flipping the supervisor card out to bog him down in work. Yesterday he missed lunch because she had him count coin bags. I think it is time for me to move out,' said Ally.

'Is that what Gavin wants?' Renee asked.

'No. At least he says he doesn't, and it is not what I want right now either. But I do not want to ruin his relationship with Deborah,' said Ally.

'Sounds like she is doing a good enough job of that herself,' said Renee.

'I know, and the best thing I can do is make friends with her. Show her I am no threat. Gavin and I are done; I just need a safe place to stay until the police capture Scott Clarke, and I can get on with my life. That is what Gavin, and I agreed to. I will try it anyway. If this doesn't work, I will have a rethink.' Ally nodded her head, agreeing with her own statement.

'Sounds like a plan. You could always move back in with us,' said Renee.

'Thanks, but I can't, you understand?' She looked at her friend.

'Just saying. We miss you. I am so happy to see you putting your life back together: yellow belt and music school are just the beginning!' Renee pulled the car into Gavin's driveway and hugged Ally around the shoulders.

'Thanks, Renee, wish me luck. I am going to have to make friends with Deb-or-aaah!'

Ally found Gavin and Deborah in the kitchen. Deborah was just about to take a sip of the pasta sauce. Ally wondered if she would also think it needed a little spice.

'Whoa, that's a lot of chilli,' said Deborah.

'Finally, you learn how to spice things up,' Ally announced herself.

'Allison, I did not know you would be home!' Deborah smiled, but the smile didn't reach her eyes.

'Why don't you join us for pasta? It is all vegetarian,' said Gavin, ignoring a glare from Deborah.

'Sure, I would love to. Just let me get changed and I will be right back.'

'How was karate?' asked Deborah.

'Karate is fantastic. Our instructor is awesome. Really big on the technicalities and art of the style, and we got our yellow belts tonight.'

'Oh, sounds interesting. What style is it?'

'Kofukan by Karate for Life. My instructor, Sensei Dan, is great!'

'Oh, do I sense a little teacher crush?' Gavin teased.

'No, don't think so, besides he is married and twice my age, but I don't doubt that he would have been a dish in his younger years.' Ally left the kitchen, calling, 'I will be right back!'

'Why do I feel you already invited her?' Deborah asked Gavin while she refilled her own wineglass, ignoring his.

'Would you have come?' he asked.

'No, I would have suggested that we go out together, alone, like we used to. This is just too weird, Gavin. I don't like it. I don't like this whole damn situation. Who are you with, who do you want to be with? You cannot continue living with a foot in both worlds.'

'For the umpteenth time, you Deborah. You are the woman that I want. Ally is like my little sister. I have no feeling here,' he moved his arm in a circular pattern over his groin. 'Nothing,' he said.

Deborah put her hand over his heart. 'Maybe not there, but this is still full of concern and misdirected love and devotion. What is in here should also be mine.' She took her hand away and picked up the bottle of Moscato to refill her drink.

'I do feel for you here too. Deborah, you know that I have feelings for you, I care deeply for you.' Standing behind her, he could see her reflection in the window, anger was furrowing her brow, but when she met his eyes and he smiled, she let herself relax as his hands tightened around her waist. 'You need to give me time Deborah, and patience. It won't be like this forever.'

'You say that but how long have I already waited for you? How long do I have to keep waiting? It is not fair. Just when I thought that you were ready to make a commitment to me you let her back in!' She took his hand from her waist and turns to face him, an inch away from his face. 'Cheaters cheat Gavin. How do I know that you are not cheating on me now?'

'Because I love you.' He shrugged.

'You love me? Are you sure?'

'Yes, I am. Now can we please have a nice dinner, and then I will drive you home?'

'I would rather you just drive me home' She smiled and kissed him on the chin.

Chapter Eight

Renee and David arrived armed with wine, a cheesecake and a farewell gift for Ally. Gavin had prepared a full four course meal to send Ally off in style.

'It's just like old times,' David said.

The gang of four feasted their way through a menu of pumpkin soup with croutons and crispy onion garnish, stuffed mushrooms, spinach pasta with three kinds of cheese, fresh fruit. and Renee's famous tiramisu cheesecake.

'A toast to Ally.' Gavin held up his glass of chardonnay. 'May you always find your way home and know that there will always be love in our hearts for you no matter how far you trail or how wide you roam.' He broke into song, 'Still call Australia home... Cheers to our girl, Ally!'

'I would like to add,' Renee said, standing for effect, 'that I will miss you terribly, and I think that it sucks that you are going on a cruise around the world and I am going on a bus trip to Adelaide to move in indefinitely with David's parents! Why couldn't Deborah's friend find me a passage to somewhere else too?'

'Hey,' said David. Renee winked in his direction and continued… 'Ally, I wish you joy, but most of all (it was Renee's turn to break into song) I wish you loooooove, and I……. I… I… will always love you…'

'Cheers!'

'Cheers!'

'Cheers!'

'Well, thank you,' said Ally, 'but that singing was truly awful, and if you ever try that again I promise that I shall never ever come home for fear that you will repeat it!'

'Oh, is that right?' Renee laughed. 'Maybe we should rethink present time and send Miss Haughty off empty handed?'

David ignored Renee and handed Ally a beautifully wrapped box. Renee was a gifted wrapper, capable of making a ceremony out of the smallest gifts.

'We are all going to miss you, Ally. It is okay with me if you don't like the singing of these two clowns,' said David.

Renee thumped his arm playfully. It hurt, and he rubbed it, seeking sympathy.

'Thank you, David, for not singing, for the present. I will miss you, all of you,' said Ally.

Ally set the box down on the table in front of her and untied the first gold ribbon, which she folded along its length and set down on the table. Gavin watched her and smiled, remembering how she always treated each gift as precious, down to the very wrapping it came in, saying that she appreciated the trouble the giver went to, in not just selecting the gift but the card and paper too. It was all part of the thoughtfulness. It reminded him of why he had loved her, and he knew that a part of him would never stop loving her. The feeling both warmed and saddened him.

Inside the box were a digital camera, travel journal, writing paper, envelopes, and a beautiful, ebony wood pen engraved with her name on it. Ally couldn't help but cry. Through the tears, she said, 'This is really too much, guys.'

Renee stood up to hug her, and the two friends sobbed in each other's arms.

'Karate classes will not be the same without you!' said Renee.

'You will keep going, won't you? Renee, you have to achieve your black belt. You are so good, way too good to quit.'

'I don't think anyone in Adelaide does karate,' she wailed.

'You keep it up or I will find you and I will kick your arse!'

'Ally,' said Gavin, his arms around both girls, 'I hate to break this up, but I have to get you to the airport.'

'Ally, I hope you don't mind if we say goodbye here, David is uncomfortable with me warbling in public. I will miss you so much, honestly, it is only just dawning on me now. You really are going, aren't you? What am I going to do without you?' Renee cried.

'You have me,' David offered, joining the ring.

'Oh, but what good are you in a crisis?' Renee smiled at him, thankful for his thoughtfulness.

'I make good cups of tea and buttered toast,' he offered, squeezing the group together in his bearlike arms.

Earlier Gavin had asked Renee and David to say their goodbyes at the house. He wanted this moment alone with Ally, but now he was here he didn't know how to say what he was feeling. He wanted to tell her how deep his feeling for her ran despite their breakup. He wanted her to know how confused he felt, but the words wouldn't come. They drove most of the way from Applecross to the airport in silence as the radio played late-night love dedications. When they exited the highway towards the airport, Ally asked Gavin to steer off to the drop-off zone.

'I am sorry Gavin; I can't handle another long goodbye. It is too hard. I know when I get back things will have changed forever between us. You and Deborah will make a life together and, of course, I could be famous.

Things would just be too weird to remain in each other's lives. Let's say goodbye here. You will always be my first love. Sorry if I am not making sense, Gavin. Thanks for everything, now please pop the boot so I can get my bags out of the car before I bawl again.' She made it through her speech very matter-of-factly despite her feelings.

'Ally there is so much I wanted to say, but I don't know where to start,' said Gavin.

'Then don't. We have already said everything we need to say to each other.' She smiled softly.

'I will always love you regardless of what changes happen in my life. You are family to me,' Gavin said.

'I will always love you too, so kiss me for the last time and say goodbye, Gavin, I am about to start a wonderful adventure. We both are.'

At the front of Perth domestic terminal Gavin held Ally in his arms; he felt her arms around his neck and kissed her softly. Re-exploring the tender contour of her mouth. His tongue flicked past her lips and teased out her tongue to dance with his amid their final union. This kiss reminded them both of their old familiar passion and the love that used to be theirs.

As she checked in her baggage, the attendant handed her a yellow envelope explaining that a young man left it, saying that he was sorry, but he could not wait any longer. Curious, Ally took the envelope over to the rows of upholstered waiting chairs-a surprise from her friends or instructions from the cruise liner? Something from Gavin? She scanned the crowded airport. Maybe he was watching her?

She gasped as she looked down at the photos in her hand. Photos from that horrible night. That horrible night that she had pushed down deep inside of her, for only her nightmares to recall. Even worse, there were photos of her in Gavin's house, at karate, rehearsals, even out shopping. Scott had been stalking her.

Sweat beaded her brow. Her stomach churned. She searched the crowds again, eyes darting to each face, looked up into the mezzanine and outside through the glass. He was here, somewhere.

Ignoring protests of impatient passengers, Ally pushed through the line and returned to the woman at the counter. Seeing her shaking, the attendant took her aside.

'Please call the police,' Ally pleaded. 'There is a man here who attacked me. He left this and he must be here, now.' Ally's hands were shaking, her skin cold and damp.

'I will call them now. I am so sorry. I had no idea. He seemed so charming. Come on, I will take you through to the first-class lounge. No one gets in there without identification. I will get security to wait with you until you are safely on your flight.' The attendant closed her desk and led Ally away from the crowds.

'Thank you. I am sorry for the trouble,' said Ally.

'You have nothing to be sorry for.'

ALLISON

A tall man in a navy-blue suit appeared next to them. He introduced himself as Mike Harkins and led Ally to the first-class lounge.

Sitting in a velour tub chair, Ally cast an eye around the room, scanning the faces.

'It is okay, you are safe here. Everyone has their identification and flight details checked before we allow them in here. Your stalker is already on our alert sheets as a wanted criminal, so he won't be getting through this security. I doubt he would have the nerve to hang around here. We have security cameras all over the place. Can I get you something to drink?' Mike talked sympathetically, and he suddenly reminded Ally of her father.

She had vague recollections of him as a child, and she remembered that fatherly look. Through the windows she could see the planes waiting on the tarmac. She wished she was one of those people rushing to and from planes, oblivious to the horrors of fear, violation, and betrayal that had become a part of her life, courtesy of Scott Clarke.

'Ally, are you okay? Can I get you something to drink?' Mike asked again.

A waft of musk, like her father.

'Sorry. No, thank you. I am fine,' she said.

'How about I get us some tea?' He didn't wait for an answer but stood up and strode to the counter to place their order.

Tea, Ally's mind shifted to tea. Why do people think tea is so special? How about a valium, a joint, a southern comfort?

Tea! How about something served with a sharp knife, a gun, an axe, or anything to protect myself? *Where is that bastard?* She thought. Her hand tightened on the yellow envelope lying across her lap.

Ally's resolve strengthened. She had to leave. No point going back. There was nowhere to turn. She needed to be away from that bastard. She still could not put into words what this meant, how she felt about how that bastard had violated her over and over, more than on that terrible night. How many times had he drugged her? Who else had seen these photos?

What about Gavin, had he seen the photos? She wanted to call him, but she couldn't. He was going straight to Deborah's. Renee and David would be in bed by now, and there was no one else. The sooner she boarded that plane and got on with her new life, the better.

Interrupting her thoughts, Mike put the tray on the table. 'Here we are. I wasn't sure if you wanted something to eat. My wife always does in a crisis, so I grabbed some vanilla slices and French fancies. Is it okay if I join you?' he asked, taking the seat across from her.

'Yes, please do, I prefer some distraction, I mean, company.' She faltered.

He set the tea down on the table in front of her and she helped herself to milk and sugar. Mike did the same and took a vanilla slice. 'I have to admit these are my favourites.' He grinned, childlike.

Ally smiled. 'My mum used to make the best ones.'

'Would you like to call her? Anyone? Here, you can use my phone,' Mike said past a mouthful of the vanilla slice.

'My mum died a few years ago. Cancer. My dad left when I was little, he met someone else.'

'Another woman? It happens a lot,' Mike said in consolation.

'A man.'

ALLISON

'Happens, maybe not so often.' Mike wiped custard from his chin with the airport napkin.

Allison watched the two policemen enter the lounge. Mike quickly wiped his hands on his napkin and offered his hand to the police sergeant.

'Gerry, how are you?' he said.

'Living the high life, I see, Mike. How are you?' said the officer.

'I am good, but no time for chitter chatter. This is Miss Allison Jones. I believe you already know of the situation?'

Ally offered a weak smile. 'Hello.'

'Good evening, Miss Jones. I am Sergeant Adams, and this is Constable Samuels. We were informed that the man, who allegedly attacked you was seen in the airport this evening and has left some photographic evidence that he has been stalking you. Is that correct?'

'There are photos in here showing occasions where I seem to be unconscious...that I have no recollection of... and this is...' Her voice broke.

'Are they the photos?' Adams asked, pointing to the envelope in Ally's hand.

'Yes. Please take them. I never want to see them again.' Ally handed them over across the table.

'Thank you. We will get them to forensics immediately. We officers police searching the area now, and airport security is on high alert,' Adams said.

'I am due to leave for Melbourne in an hour. I must be there to meet the Star Princess. I am a singer on that liner, and I have to go. Please don't tell me that I can't go!' she pleaded.

'You can go, you have done nothing wrong,' said Adams.

'Thank you.' She exhaled.

'But stay in touch, you may be required to give evidence.' Constable Samuels spoke for the first time.

'Will I have to come back?' she asks.

'No, we can arrange to speak to you from anywhere in the world,' Adams said.

'What if he has already left? What if he is on a plane right now out of Perth, he has been watching me, he knows what I am doing, and he could follow me around the world.' Ally paled as her voice drifted. Her trembling hands shook against the second cup of tea Mike poured her. She automatically sipped. It was lukewarm, sweet, and thick with tannin.

The three men exchanged a look of concern. Ally could be right. Even with police manning the exits. Mistakes happened, and slime could slink through.

The boarding call for flight QF568 sounded. 'Can passengers please proceed to gate four for boarding,' said the voice over the speaker.

'That's me.' Ally stood and collected her bags.

'We will escort you to the gate, and perhaps Mike can stay on board with you?' Adam offered, looking to Mike for confirmation.

'Yes, of course, I will get the boss to sort it out while we are on our way to the gate.'

Like a presidential detail the three men flanked Ally. Mike led them towards the departure gate talking in his walkie talkie all the way. The sergeant carried her overnight bag. It was surreal to Ally, walking through a nightmare flanked by her soldiers, strangers. Building a wall between her and who knew what. But Ally knew. She knew more than enough to be afraid.

All four scanned the crowd looking for signs; a tourist snapped the procession in case it was someone famous with her entourage.

ALLISON

They stride past the other passengers and boarded the half-filled plane. The two police officers assessed the passengers while Mike spoke briefly to the flight attendant.

Bidding farewell to the officers, Ally thanked them for their help, and they promised her that they would do everything to find him and that they were leaving her in good hands. Mike led Ally into first class.

'We've had you upgraded. You will be more comfortable here. Maybe get some rest?'

'Thank you.' Ally collapsed into the seat he offered her by the window.

A flight attendant appears with hot towels, nuts, and orange juice. 'Thank you.' Ally accepted absently. *Some adventure this is turning out to be.*

She looked out the small porthole window, saw her patent red crocodile look suitcase on top of a pile of luggage being put onto the plane.

Then him.

She blinked hard. Unable to speak, she grabbed Mike's arm and pointed to the man below on the tarmac. He was wearing the blue uniform of the airport ground crew, he was staring up at her. Mike was on his handheld radio giving the all-out alert, describing Scott, his clothing, and his position.

'Oh god he is trying to find a way onto the plane!'

She said. 'What if he gets on to the plane?'

'I have a gun, Ally. I will shoot him,' Mike assured her. As the plane taxied to the runway, the police ploughed Scott Clarke onto the tarmac, cuffed him, and led him away.

Chapter Nine

Ally paused on the dock to take a photograph of the postcard scene in front of her as the Star Princess rocked gently at the dock's edge. It was tethered by thick, coarse ropes to the cleat on the dock. Bunting trailed across the ship from port to starboard, brightly polished portholes gleamed in the morning sun. The crew dressed in their blue-and-white uniforms were scurrying all over the ship. A staff gangplank stood off to the side of the wide, steel-gated gangplank used by paying guests. Ally's entrance was barely two feet wide and little more than a plank of wood resting between the kitchen door and the dock. An overworked kitchen aid directed her to the personnel department. She dragged her case and overnight bag along the corridor behind her. Ally was soon lost despite the ship's map in her hand.

'Do you need some help?' came a voice behind her. 'Yes, please, I am so completely lost,' Ally said, turning to the voice.

ALLISON

The woman behind her wore a velour track suit, her red hair exploded in a mass of curls to frame her freckled face.

'Hi, I'm Cheryl, first time on the ship?'

Ally nodded. 'My name is Ally; I'm supposed to be reporting to personnel.'

'You must be the new singer? I hope you have more luck than the old one.' Cheryl tilted her head to the side.

Ally nodded. 'What happened to the old singer?'

'Fell overboard, he was drunk. I am the dance instructor; I get to teach the old folks the merengue and the waltz. The pay is lousy, but the tips! Come on, I will take you to the old hag,' said Cheryl in her sing song voice.

'Old hag?' Ally asked.

'Yes, that's our pet name for personnel. She can come across as a bit of a bitch, but don't take it personally.' Cheryl knocked on the door.

'Come in,' said a sharp voice from behind the door.

Cheryl opened the door wide. 'Hello, Paula, nice to see you again. I am here for my room assignment, and this is Ally, our new singer.'

'Nice to meet you, Ally. I have heard a lot about you, and I am looking forward to seeing your show.' Paula eyed them both over the top of her brass-rimmed glasses.

'Thank you,' Ally said.

'You are both assigned to level five cabin six. I am sure that you can find it, Cheryl. Here are your welcome aboard packs, ladies. The usual is in there - sickness pills, employment contracts, room keys, and so on. If you have any questions, my door is always open. Figuratively speaking, that is.' Paula waved them both away and returned to the business on her desk.

'Thank you.' Ally clutched the envelope and followed Cheryl from the tiny office.

The cabin was small, with a set of bunks along one wall. A little vanity had two cupboards on either side for them to hang their clothes in, and there was a tiny bathroom with a toilet and shower. Everything had been meticulously downsized.

'Well, this is home sweet home to South Hampton.' Ally heaved her case onto her bunk.

'South Hampton? You are not going all the way around then?' asked Cheryl.

'No, my contract ends in England. I plan to stay and work around there for a while. Maybe even Europe? Then when I can, I hope to gain another liner contract going who knows where,' said Ally.

'Good luck to you. I get homesick. It is amazing how good it feels after four months at sea to sleep in my own bed again. Don't you think you will be homesick?'

'Home.' Ally said the word as if it belonged to a foreign language. 'I don't really know where that is anymore.'

Day three at sea, the ship was heading for Christchurch, and the floating hotel was a hive of activity, holiday makers and workers alike settling into their sea legs. Ally's sea sickness had hit within the first few hours of setting sail, and she was grateful for the personnel's welcome pack. Rehearsals were starting today, and she was feeling well enough to attend them.

Ally met her band in the concert theatre to run over the playlist for the first show. It included songs from Judy Garland, Frank Sinatra, Nat King Cole, and a few Peggy Lee numbers she had snuck in for good measure. The smell of the place was familiar: old beer and tobacco, stale sweat, and stuffy night club air. Ally

ALLISON

started to relax. She was making new friends among the crew, enjoyed dinners in the mess, and relished the family atmosphere the company surrounded her with. For the first time in months, she no longer had to look over her shoulder, but she still insisted that they lock the cabin door each night, even while her roommate kept losing her key and woke her at odd hours. Cheryl was a fun roommate; honest, quirky, and on the run from something she wasn't ready to talk about, but Ally was okay with Cheryl keeping secrets, she was good at doing so too.

When the ship pulled away from Christchurch Ally and her band began their first show. A dedication to the divas of croon. Singing *'Somewhere Over the Rainbow'* in her silver mesh dress, her hair swept up in a French twist and her mother's diamante earrings, she looked every inch an old-time starlet. The audience was a sea of grey hair, Grecian two thousand, and the odd bad topaz. They soaked up every note she sang. For the encore, Ally belted out Ella's *'Hit the Road Jack'*; they got the cheeky message and applauded louder. On a performance high, Ally gave her band a high-five before they all headed to the mess hall for drinks.

Chapter Ten

Ready for an adventure, Ally left the ship early on the morning of their arrival in Osaka. Sensei Dan had inspired a fascination with all things Japan, and he had recommended that she see the Kinkakuji Temple. She had nabbed a place on a tour bus, filled to the brim with Silver Hairs. The Silver Hairs were a group of sixty-plus adventurers taking on any challenge the Star Princess could muster. Ally wanted their enthusiasm and love of life to rub off on her.

The bus weaved its way through Tempozan before taking the motorway past the city of Osaka through green hills and rice fields to Kinkaku-ji and its golden temple, Kinkaku. An animated Japanese tour guide led the group around the temple, when Ally's camera caught a familiar figure in the viewfinder.

'Ally?'

'Robert! Oh my god, it is you.'

ALLISON

The two hugged, attracting the attention of the Silver Hairs around them.

'What are you doing here?' they asked in unison.

'Sorry, you first,' said Robert.

'I am working my way to the United Kingdom on the Star Princess. I sing in the cabaret, what about you?' she asked.

'My brother is getting married. I am here on a two-day stopover on my way to England. Ally, any chance we can spend the day together?' he asked.

'Sure, I would like that. Just let me tell William so he doesn't worry,' Ally said.

'William? I didn't mean to intrude, if you are with some- one...'

'No, William is my tour buddy,' Ally laughed.

Robert smiled. Here was the girl who had stolen his heart. Arm in arm, they strolled around the botanical gardens that shaded the temple.

'Robert, I am sorry for not calling you back like I had promised. Things were not good for me at the time, and I just didn't think it would be right to drag you through it too,' said Ally.

'Ally, I know what happened before. I could kill him. I can't believe that the police had him, lost him, and the last thing I heard was they were still searching for him. In Queensland. They suspect he stole a car and headed across the centre,' said Robert.

Ally watched Robert's mouth as the words came out. 'Had him? I was at the airport when they caught him, I saw him pinned to the tarmac. What the hell happened?'

'I am sorry, Ally, I assumed you knew. He shot a policeman. He can't hurt you, Ally. He has no idea where you are, and besides, those Silver Hairs you roll with look pretty scary!' Robert said, putting his arm around her. Robert held her tight against his chest, and he planted a gentle kiss on the top of her head.

Ally remembered how he had made her feel before, she remembered the warmth and love and wanting. She returned the embrace; wrapping her arms around his waist, she raised her head to meet his lips in their second kiss. Their lips gently parted.

He had the power to take away her pain, her fear. At that moment, all she felt was love, all she saw was a future. Deep inside her, she felt a longing that had not stirred since their first kiss.

'Where is your next port sailor?' Robert asked.

'Nagasaki, in two days, Captain,' she said.

He smiled, and taking her hand in his the two began the climb up the carved stone stairway to the lookout over Kyoto.

Chapter Eleven

The anticipation was palpable. Ally was excited when the ship finally pulled into port at Nagasaki. She scanned the dock for Robert as the ship inched its way closer to land. She began waving frantically when she spotted him.

'Is that him? The hunk who followed you all the way from Australia. It looks like he is coming aboard.' Cheryl teased Ally.

'Don't get ahead of yourself, he has to be in England for a wedding soon,' said Ally.

'Whatever you say, but that looks like a suitcase to me. I'd say he is coming on board! I bet that man would follow you anywhere.'

When the gang planks were in place, Robert walked on to the ship. A ship porter was carrying his suitcase.

Ally rushed to meet him. 'Are you being deported?'

'No, and I will turn around now and never bother madam again if she would rather I didn't,' he said.

'Didn't what?' she asked.

'Didn't want me on the ship with her. I have booked a cabin to Phuket. I will have to fly from there to make it to Kevin's wedding on time, but I really wanted to...'

Ally didn't let him finish. She wrapped her arms around his neck, and he met her kiss with relief. Robert enveloped her in his arms.

'Ahem.' The porter coughed behind them.

'Sorry,' Ally said, pulling away first, 'you will want to get him checked in. He is all yours, for now.'

'Thank you,' the porter nodded.

'You have a bath! Do you know how long it has been since I have had a bath?' Ally was turning circles in Robert's bathroom.

'Well, I was going to say something about that.' Robert laughed as she playfully punched his arm. 'You are welcome to enjoy the bath any time. I promise to be the perfect gentleman. Look, they have all these soaps and smelly things for you too.' He held up a basket of Crabtree toiletries the liner reserved for first-class passengers.

'This must have cost you a fortune,' she said.

He shrugged. 'Let's get out of here and take in some sights. It would be a shame to leave without at least taking in the view from Mt Inasa.'

The Silver Hair bus wound its way through Nagasaki while the petite guide pointed out the local attractions and explained some of the history of the area in a clear but broken English accent. Ally and Robert sat at the back of the bus, holding hands. The bus drove over Megami Bridge and onto the Nagasaki Atomic Bomb Museum. Ally and Robert left the tour here.

ALLISON

In the afternoon, they walked side by side through the Peace Garden. Despite the chill they explored every corner of the memorial, stopping for a warming green tea before heading to Mt Inasa for a cable car ride at sunset to see the city lights of Nagasaki.

Back on board the ship, Ally felt strange sitting in the main dining room surrounded by co-workers. She did not know them all by name but recognised many faces from the staff mess hall.

'Is something wrong Ally?' Robert took her hand. 'You look nervous, and beautiful too.'

'What if they think I have just hooked up with you on board? It's a little Pretty Woman...' she whispered across the table.

'If it bothers you, we could eat in my room and I could have some strawberries and champagne sent up?'

'No, that would be worse.'

'Well, let them gossip. I will happily set anyone straight that dares to ask me.' Robert sat back in his chair.

'Defend my honour, will you?'

'Without limits, my lady.' He bowed his head and held his hand over his heart.

'This is really a beautiful room. I feel like I am on the love boat.' Her cheeks flushed. 'You know, because of the style.'

'Ally, I want you to know that I have strong feelings for you. The more time I spend with you, the more I have to be with you. No one has ever had that effect on me before. I hope I am not coming on too strong. I will follow your lead, Ally, fast or slow, whatever you need. I just ask that we try to see where we can go. I guess what I am trying to say is that I don't want to say goodbye to you when I leave this ship.' Robert exhaled. He was relieved at having finally said what was on his mind.

'Robert, I am not sure what to say other than…'

Robert interrupted her. 'I spoke too soon. Please forget I said anything.'

'No, you misunderstand me, I would like that very much too.'

'Thank god! I thought I had buggered things up. You looked like you were ready to jump ship.'

They held hands across the white linen tablecloth, and Robert ordered another round of drinks in celebration.

After Ally's show, Robert and Ally walked along the deck. A soft breeze cooled their skin as they gazed out on a starlit night over the Pacific Ocean. 'Thank you for the song dedication, no one has ever done that for me before. Makes a bloke feel special.'

'That was my intention.' Ally turned to face him, lifted her arms around his neck, and tilted her head to meet his lips. They pulled each other close. His hardness was on her belly. Her tongue explored his mouth. His hand was in her hair. Ally's hand slid down the curve of his back to pull him into her, grasping his buttocks.

A soft moan escaped his lips. Ally's lips were soft and full. Her nipples were hard through her soft, satin gown. Robert had been nursing a semi hard-on for most of the day. Her red-hot, satin dress fitted to the curves of her beautiful body; her smell, her taste, and the way she looked at him across that room when she sang made him harder still. Robert was falling in love with her, and he wanted her to feel the same way.

'Let's go to your room, Robert. We are creating a scene out here.' Ally pulled away from him and led him back into the ship towards his cabin.

At the door to his cabin, he turned to her. 'Are you sure, Ally? Please don't feel pressured because of what I said earlier. I will happily wait a hundred lifetimes for you.' He touched the softness of her cheek with his fingertips.

'Get the bloody door open. I am all hot and bothered now, and need to use your bathroom.' Ally puts his hand to her lips and planted a kiss on his fingertips.

'Thank god,' said Robert, opening the door.

Ally emerged from the bathroom to find Robert making them both gin and tonic. 'There's no lemon,' he said.

Ally shrugged, reached behind her, and unzipped the red, satin dress. She drew it from her shoulders and dropped it on the floor. She was wearing a matching, mid-thigh camisole. She stepped out of her shoes as she walked towards him.

Robert took off his tie, threw it onto the couch. Ally waited a foot away while he unbuttoned his shirt. His muscular chest was blanketed in soft, curly hair. She stepped forward to explore the landscape with her hands, then with her mouth she kissed across from one pink nipple to the next.

Robert moaned Ally. His cock pulsed and pushed hard against his trousers, wanting attention. His shirt dropped to the floor. Ally took off his belt, letting his pants join it. She stepped back and smiled. He stepped out of his shoes and clothes, naked except for black tented briefs.

He moved towards her and cupped her face in his hands, kissing her deeply. She pulled him towards the bed. Robert helped her slide her camisole over her head. He explored her body softly with kisses, returning to her mouth gently. Hungry for him, she answers by kissing him deeper. She groaned as he kissed her neck and then moved down to the valley of her breasts. Ally arched her back, giving herself to him. He eagerly took one breast, then the other into his mouth, he nibbled, and he teased with his tongue, moving from one breast then the other. Ally was wet, she wanted him deep inside of her.

Her pulse quickened as one of his hands moved lower into her panties. Rubbing along the sleek wetness of her desire he found her entrance and pushed first one, then two fingers deep inside to explore her. Her back arched to meet his hand. He kissed her soft lips while his fingers instinctively brought her to climax. Her tight muscles clamped down around his fingers and he wants to be inside her.

Ally lowered her panties. Robert took the cue and removed his own, letting his cock spring free. Ally kicked her panties off as she wrapped a hand around the width of him, feeling him become even harder. She gently squeezed the silky soft hard texture of him. She pulled him gently as he positioned himself above her. Ally guided him into her folds. Wet slickness clamped tight around him, squeezing him as he pushed slowly inside her.

Their eyes locked. Robert was struggling to constrain himself. He slowed down to follow Ally's lead. Each time Ally pushed back at him he pumped a little harder. He kissed her mouth, her neck and made his way back to her right nipple. He took the pink rose bud into his mouth, grazed it with his teeth, teasing it harder with his tongue. Ally's hands were stretched above her head, gripping the ornate bars of the bedhead. She surrendered to her body, to the pleasure he was giving her.

They responded quicker to each other. Blood racing, pumping. Orgasm took over every inch of Ally's body. It tore open her heart and mind as he pierced her flesh with his. Colours flashed before her eyes and for a moment she saw them on the bed together. She saw his arse tense, the shape of his legs, his feet pushing into the mattress, the ripples of his muscular back. She saw the slightest hint of a tan line at the back of his neck onto which her hand was now clutching.

She shuddered as she held onto him. Feeling him explode inside her, his cock pulsated and filled her. 'Oh my god,' gasped Robert before his head collapsed into the nook of her neck.

'I am falling in love with you. I have never, had a day like this before and I never want to think of a day when I am not with the woman who is solely responsible for giving this day to me. Thank you, Ally, for giving us a chance.'

'You are very, very welcome,' Ally breathed.

Robert lay down next to Ally. She turned on her side away from him so that she nestled her back against his torso. Spent, he snuggled up behind her, one arm around her body. He pulled her into him, and they slept, without stirring until morning.

The next eight days sped by. The lovers filled them with sightseeing in Xingang, Halong Bay and Sihanoukville. There were afternoon siestas and long lunches, both in and out of doors. At night, they created future memories to hold on to during lonely times, when circumstances kept them apart. Robert watched in admiration as Ally entertained the passengers.

Afterwards, they would have a drink and sometimes stay back for a dance or two before, heading back to his cabin.

Robert's departure that had been looming above them swiftly arrived. Ally collected the clothes and makeup items she had left in his cabin over the last eight days and took them back to her own cabin.

When she returned, she found Robert on the balcony. He had arranged for them to be eating a champagne brunch as the ship pulled into shore. They sat across from each other at the table, and Robert put a long velvet box in front of Ally.

'Just a small token of my feelings for you. I hope you like it.' He smiled as she opened the box.

'A pearl bracelet! I love it. You shouldn't have, but thank you, I really love it,' she said. He left his seat to help her place the antique bracelet around her wrist.

'The jeweller promised me that it was a genuine antique from the Xia Dynasty.' Robert kissed her as the croissants and fresh fruit arrived.

Ally pulled away to clear her throat. 'Sorry.'

'You look a little pale, could you be coming down with something? Maybe you should take it easy while I am gone,' said Robert.

'I am okay, but I think you may be right. I've been burning the candles at both delicious ends, and I think it's taken a toll. I do feel like I am coming down with a cold, my throat is feeling a little off. Don't worry I will get some rest, take some honey, ginger and lemon and have an early night straight after the show,' said Ally.

'You better. I don't want to hear you have been partying all night with the senior citizens.' Robert said, smiling and taking his seat across from her.

'Scouts honour, I promise.'

It was a long walk for them down the gangplank. Their farewell kiss held up the sightseeing passengers without complaint. Love was in the air.

'You have twelve sleeps to get better. Promise me that you will take care of yourself. I love you, Ally.'

'I love you too, Robert. I am so happy that we have found each other again.'

Chapter Twelve

Waking from a nap later that day, Ally had just enough time to dress and get to the show. Her voice was husky, so the band threw in a few extended lead breaks and instrumentals. At the end of their session, she thanked the guys for helping her out before skipping on having drinks and leaving for an early night.

The next morning, her throat was worse. She thought it was best to fight off a simple cold with another day's rest in bed. Cheryl fetched a regular supply of warm honey and lemon drinks from the kitchen and coaxed Ally to take sips between naps.

At seven o'clock, Ally struggled to get ready for the show. Her skin was clammy, and her head spun. Ally's fiery throat hurt. When Jimmy, the band's lead guitarist, saw her backstage, he ordered her to see the doctor before she infected them all. She obeyed and went straight to the infirmary.

Following an examination of the doctor said, 'I think we have more than a cold, it could be strep, I'll send a swab to the lab in Colombo to be sure. Meanwhile, take two capsules three times a day, preferably with food if you can manage it. They are broad-spectrum antibiotics so, they should help, and I will give you some painkillers to ease that sore throat. I will let personnel know that you will not be on duty for the next few days. Singing with a throat as red and swollen as yours might cause permanent damage to your voice and throat. It is just not worth it Ally.'

'You are the expert,' she sighed 'I hope this does not blow my chances of getting another contract.'

'You are a great singer, and the crew and passengers all love you. Don't worry, just rest and get better. I expect to see you here again at ten in the morning to see how you are doing and if the antibiotics are working.'

'Okay, thank you.' Ally spoke softly and left taking her bottle of antibiotics and a box of pain relievers with her.

In the cabin, Cheryl was nowhere to be seen. She was spending more and more time in the sous-chef's accommodation. Love was definitely in the air. Ally took a hot shower, took her medicine and tucked herself tight under the covers of her single ship bunk bed. She was happy that Robert was not here to see her in such a state, but she missed him all the same.

On his plane to Heathrow, Robert felt like a man who had everything. It had to be fate. How else could you explain him meeting the girl he had fallen in love with at a party in Perth in Osaka, Japan? Surely the universe had a divine plan for them to be together. As soon as she arrives in London, I will ask her to marry me. He smiled to himself like a fool. The flight attendant came

ALLISON

down the centre line of the airplane, offering reading material to passengers. Robert took a West Australian News to pass the time.

The front-page headline read "Couple Tortured by Rapist" and underneath was a picture of Renee and David on the beach, smiling into the camera. Ally's best friend was dead. He had no way of knowing if she knew. Reading on the couple were found dead by a real estate agent. Both had been sexually assaulted, bound, and gagged. Various Polaroids were found in the house and their blood had been used to write "Allison" across the walls. All evidence pointed to Scott Clarke. The suspect was still at large. Robert folded the paper and set it down on the empty seat next to him. He needed to contact Ally. She would need him by her side.

Ally was exhausted. The pain killer's Dr Allen had given her had knocked her out halfway through writing a song for Robert. She tossed and turned, the fever burning. Sweat stained her nightie, her sheets, and blankets. She woke in a half daze, shivering from cold. She pulled off the damp bedding and climbed back onto her bed and into her dreams.

In her dream, she was watching herself singing at a talent contest in the cabaret lounge of the Raffles Hotel back in Perth. Ally had lost to a contortionist in a G-string. 'Hardly decent!' her mother had complained at the time. 'You showed real talent; you're not just some freak of nature.' They had laughed at the ridiculousness of it and Ally had never entered another competition.

Now, she was back there with her mother. She wanted to stay in the memory, but her fevered mind tossed her over to Gavin and the night of their breakup. She watched herself crying. A giant heart breaking above their heads, crashing down on them both, their little house filled with red, swallowing them both. She cried out in her sleep. Her mother came back and took her down a long dark corridor. Decaying limbs reached from the walls, heavy breathing filled her ears and, a voice spoke of evil. Scott's voice! Arms gripped her throat and pinned her to the wall. Scott's laughter rang in the darkness. 'You will never escape. I will do things to you that will make sure Robert will never touch you again!'

'No!' Ally's thrashing was useless. 'No!' Ally woke screaming. She told herself that she was okay, it was just the fever. She drank some water, took more medication and crawled back into bed. The fever continued tormenting her through the night.

Dr Allen knocked on Ally's door at eleven thirty, a little concerned that she hadn't been to his office as instructed. He could hear Ally coughing on the other side of the door. When she didn't answer the door after he knocked several times and called her name, he called for housekeeping to unlock the cabin with the master key.

He found Ally in her bunk. She had vomited onto her pillow. The mess of it was on her pyjamas and clumped in her hair. He checked her pulse and tried to rouse her by calling her name. The thermometer showed forty-three degrees. She was wet through.

'Dr Allen,' said Ally coming to, 'please help me I think I am losing my mind. The seagulls have taken over the messes,' she drifted back.

'Ally,' he persisted. 'I need you to wake up, I need you to stay with me.' He laid her down in the mess on her mattress and started the shower running.

'What are you doing?' Cheryl was at the door.

'Thank goodness. Quick, I need your help, we have to get her in the shower, she is running a high fever and we need to get it under control now!'

Cheryl saw that her roommate looked ghastly, vomit was clumped in her hair, dark shadows circled her eyes, her nightie was wet through. Ally was shivering.

'What do you need me to do?' said Cheryl.

'I think it would be more appropriate for you to undress her, Here put this towel over her and I will carry her through into the bathroom,' he said.

'God, the prudish English, and you are a doctor? What is wrong with her?'

'I thought it was strep throat. I will get the results from Colombo when we dock. She is on a broad-spectrum antibiotic, but I am just guessing at this stage. If the cause is viral the medicine won't do a thing. What is more important now is that we stop her temperature from rising, we must get it under control.'

Cheryl dodged a punch Ally threw out blindly. Ally rolled over onto her stomach. Cheryl tried to remove her pants, only to be struck with a foot directly into her abdomen. The blow winded Cheryl, and she doubled over and hit the floor.

'Are you all right?' Dr Allen helped her stand up. 'Breathe deeply.'

'Ouch, I think she broke a rib,' Cheryl gasped.

'You can still talk so that means, nothing is broken, you are okay. Let me sort Ally out first and then we will look at your ribs and tape them up if need be.' he said.

He stood holding Ally in the shower under the tepid water. 'It's okay Ally, you are safe, we are here to help you. I will help you fight the fever,' Dr Allen used a sponge to clean her face and hands and ran water over her hair.

In Ally's fevered mind, she saw her father. She was just a little girl in a hospital recovering from pneumonia.

Her dad was reading her the story of Snow White and she was sad because Snow White's mother had died leaving her alone with her father and evil stepmother. Her father laughed and promised that they would never leave her, that they loved her and when she got better, they would buy her a pony. A hundred ponies appeared in her dream, filling the room and her father disappeared. She called for her mother, but her mother didn't come. Then she saw the ocean. Water drew her in, and she floated, her body caressed by the ebb and flow. She wanted to fight the blackness.

Cheryl stood in the doorway. 'She has some kick in her. How is she doing?'

'Better, calmer anyway. Are you alright?' He looked at Cheryl.

'Yeah, no worse than the flogging I got as a kid. What are we going to do now?'

'Can you get the gurney from the infirmary and bring it here? I think it is better to isolate her until we find out what is causing the infection. It will be easier for me to treat her there too; she could be like this for days.'

'I am on my way,' said Cheryl, turning to leave the room. Ally woke in a pool of her own sweat. She tried to sit up, but she could not get her muscles to obey. She was attached to a beeping machine with flashing lights. A bottle hung upside down on a stand next to her bed. *Oh, that's right,* she thought. *I am in the hospital. I wonder where my daddy went.*

Four days out of Southampton, Ally was still shifting in and out of consciousness. The tests had come back positive for

ALLISON

bacterial strep. The intravenous antibiotics had slowly started to take effect until fluid had filled her lungs. Dr Allen had then treated her for pneumonia after picking up yet more medication in Dubai. Ally was his sole patient. Occasionally he would be given some respite by a friend of Ally's, bringing flowers, cards, even gifts. Her room was beginning to look like the ship's gift shop. He was glad of the chance to shower, change his clothes, and have a bite. When on duty, he watched Ally toss and turn, yelling out in the night. He wondered what tormented her so. She was so young, and he hoped her demons were fictional, created by the fever, but experience had taught him that fever unleashes the unconscious, unleashes past torment.

'Where am I?' Ally croaked.

'Hey, welcome back,' said Dr Allen.

'How did I get here? How long have I been…?' She tried to sit up.

'I brought you here with Cheryl. We found you in quite a state; you have been a very ill, young lady.'

'What is wrong with me?' she whispered.

'Try not to talk too much.' He handed her a cup of water with a straw to sip. 'Rest your voice. You have had a nasty case of strep, which is what I suspected ten days ago.'

'Ten days!' she squeaked.

'Hush. Yes, ten days ago. Rest your voice; you have been very ill. Your strep infection developed into pneumonia, and I had to aspirate your right lung. Your rib will be a little sore but not as sore as poor Cheryl's, but I will let her tell you all about that.' Dr Allen smiled at Ally.

Ally looked around the room. She took in the gifts, balloons, fruit baskets, get-well cards, flowers, and two teddy bears, one blue with a guitar, the other pink with a microphone.

'Where did all this come from?' she whispered.

'Your fans. They have been taking it in turns to come and sit with you. They have read and talked to you, and sometimes they have just sat and held your hand. You have made quite an impression. They will be glad to hear that you are awake. We are due to dock in Southampton tomorrow afternoon, and I have arranged for an ambulance to transport you to South Hampton General.'

'That is not necessary, is it? What if I promise to get some bed rest?'

'Sorry, Ally, I am still very concerned about your throat, and the fever has knocked you around quite a lot.

'But, doc, I have to meet someone.'

'Robert?'

'How do you know about Robert?' Ally blushed.

'You talk in your sleep, and Cheryl filled me in on the rest.'

'How is it going to look if I am carted away in an ambulance?'

'Better than a hearse,' he said.

Chapter Thirteen

The passengers were already disembarking when Robert arrived on the dock. Cheryl made her way through the crowd to meet him.

'Robert!' she called from a few feet away. 'Ally is okay, but she fell ill just after you left the ship at Phuket. She has spent all her time in the infirmary and was in and out of consciousness for over a week. Dr Allen is having her transported by ambulance to the hospital, don't panic, she is in good hands.'

'Does she know about her friends from Perth? They were killed.'

'What? No, not that I know of! The ship has had some issues with communication since China, and Ally has been ill since Thailand, so I doubt she knows anything. How awful to lose your friend. The kid has already been through the ringer. I'm glad you are here, she will need you now,' said Cheryl, shaking her head.

'Where have they taken her?' he asked.

'To Southampton General. She is so looking forward to seeing you, but more than a little pissed that the captain had her shipped off as soon as we docked, so away with you, I have my man to find. Good luck with everything, I am sorry.'

She left Robert amongst the crowd with Ally's red croc wheelie case, a crowd of happy reunions taking place around him. *I wish that I had never left her side. How am I going to tell her?*

Ally lay on the hospital bed in her own private room, courtesy of the Star Princess's health plan. Robert was at the side of her bed; he bent down to kiss her, to breathe life back into her. A gentle kiss burdened with the load he carried. 'You look awful,' he said.

'Thank you very much, my stylist just quit.' Ally smiled, taking him in. 'I take it Cheryl found you?'

'She did. I have your case in the car. I wasn't sure if you needed it here, or if I should take it back to our hotel?'

'Our hotel?' She liked the sound of it.

'We have some catching up to do when you get out of here. This hospital is not the cheeriest place to start your UK tour.'

It wasn't. The walls were a muted apricot, the commercial linoleum floors were worn, the beds looked like something from the second world war. Floral curtains hung at the window, and the air was ripe with vomit and disinfectant.

'Our hotel is much nicer than here. You can see Big Ben from our balcony. When can I sweep you away from all of this?'

'Good afternoon, Mr. and Mrs. Jones,' said the white-coated man at the door.

'I am Dr Patel,' he said, smiling at the pair. 'Dr Allen has asked me to take over your care, Allison. He is concerned that your throat infection might be caused by something more sinister than a bacterial infection, so we will run more tests to be sure and then perhaps if all is okay you can go home tomorrow.' A nurse arrived to take Ally to radiography for a chest scan and suggested that Robert get himself a cup of tea while he waited.

'Dr Patel, can I ask you something?' said Robert as Ally left the room.

He looked at Ally's file. 'That scan is just a precaution because of the pneumonia, nothing to worry about, Mr. Jones.'

'It's Robert. Doctor, please just call me Robert. I have some terrible news to tell Ally, and I worry about the effect the news will have on her.'

'Please do not tell me you are having an affair, too much love is lost because of cheating husbands.'

'No! It is nothing like that. I could never leave her. I love her; that is what makes this so hard. Two of her friends were murdered back in Australia. The killer assaulted Ally and left her for dead six months ago. He has escaped custody, and the police still have no clue where he is.'

'That is a lot to take. When is the funeral?'

'I believe that Renee's family has arranged a funeral for next Friday. That's in nine days. Do you think that Ally will be okay to travel?'

'I feel you must tell her soon and prepare to attend the funeral. She might never forgive you for letting her miss the funeral of her best friends. I know my wife wouldn't.' He smiled sympathetically. 'I do not envy you the task that lies ahead of you. Perhaps you should get yourself that tea?'

It was a cold, wet morning when Robert drove Ally along the A27 to their hotel overlooking Central London. While she showered,

Robert ordered some breakfast and tea. He sat across the table from her, taking her hand. 'Ally, it is good to be with you again.'

'Yes, I feel the same, but you are not going to propose to me now, are you?'

'Eventually, yes, but right now I have something to tell you.'

'Can it wait until after I call Renee and let her know that I have arrived safely? I promised. I have been out of touch for so long. I can't wait to tell her all about us.'

'Ally.' He responded firmly.

'Robert, what is wrong? You are scaring me, what is going on?'

Robert looked into her deep, shadow-ringed eyes, and wondered how much more she was expected to take.

'Ally, I have to tell you something,' he started.

'God, are you breaking up with me?' She asked, confused at what he could be about to tell her.

'There is no easy way to say this. Renee and David were found dead in their house. Scott Clarke killed them.' He folded her into his arms as she collapsed against him.

'Dead.' She whispered the word into his chest.

'My love, I am so sorry. I have been in contact with Renee's mum.'

'Oh god, poor Hillary.'

'The funeral is next week. We can be on a plane back to Perth in the morning.' He held her and laid a kiss on the soft silkiness of her hair before pulling her off the chair and carrying her like a child to the four-poster bed. He placed her down between the blankets, tucked her in securely, and moved in behind her, wrapping his arms around her, encasing her with his body as her tears fell.

ALLISON

After several hours of grief, Ally slept. Robert phoned the airline and booked them two first-class tickets to Perth, leaving Heathrow Airport at 10 a.m. Tuesday. After a short lay over in Dubai, they would be back in Perth on Thursday.

Ally heard Robert on the phone. Her best friend was gone. Her heart felt crushed. Tears formed a hard ball in her throat; her breath came out in hiccups. Robert ran to her and put his arms tight around her, trying to build a fortress between her and the pain. 'It is all right, Ally, it is going to be okay. I love you,' he soothed.

Ally wanted to tell him that it was not okay, but the sound of his voice soothed her, and she found it hard to imagine her life without him. Where did she find him, how would she survive without him? When did she become so weak?

Chapter Fourteen

Heavy rain fell on the stretched, black cars carrying the bodies and family of Renee and David as they moved away from the church.

'I wonder if anyone had thought about Renee's wishes? Did they think that because they died together that Renee would be happy to spend eternity with him?

Didn't they know he wasn't her perfect match, that she had no intention of living the rest of her life with him, that they forced her to? Why didn't they ask her? David could have gone back to Adelaide with his parents. Why didn't they ask her?' said Ally.

'I imagine no one had time to put much thought into it. But they did love each other.' Robert offered.

Ally nodded.

The ball in her throat tightened as the tears fell. Robert reached his arm around her, and she fell into his warm embrace. He held an umbrella over her head throughout the service, steered her through the gaps among the puddles, opened the car door, and clicked on her seat belt. He never questioned her refusal to go to the wake.

At Robert's house in South Perth, she sat near the bay window overlooking the Jacarandas. On the nearby river she watched the boats bouncing on the grey waters. Robert brought her tea and cake on a tray. Ally drank the tea in silence, his body warm against hers.

Her voice was weak. 'Robert, thank you for taking care of me, but...'

'But nothing, Ally. I intend to always be here for you.'

'You don't have to feel sorry for me, to feel obligated...'

He cut her off. 'Obligated? Ally, I have waited such a long time to be with you. Every day after that night when we first kissed, I tried to find a way to get back into your life. First, I felt I had to give you the distance you needed to get over Gavin, so I waited. I regret waiting, but you told me you needed space. I wanted to do what I thought you wanted me to do. I waited. Then that bastard hurt you and you needed time to heal, so I waited again. Then I heard you had left on a cruise, that you had gone away without a second thought of me. I had no idea where you had gone, that you would be in Osaka, and there I found you. Ally, I cannot, I will not, wait anymore. Unless you want me to leave, I will stay. I will do anything to make you happy. I will do anything to keep you safe, but I will not wait. I will not walk away from you when there is even a glimmer of hope that you want me, need me, and maybe love me.'

'I do love you, Robert, but everything is wrong,' she whispered.

'Everything is not wrong. We are perfect together.' He wrapped his arms around her, and she turned to meet his lips. The two lovers kissed for the first time since returning to West Australia. It was a long, luxurious kiss.

'Make love to me, Robert. I want to feel real again.'

Looking deep into her eyes, he picked her up and carried her to the bedroom. Her arms were looped around his neck, her fingers in his hair. She kissed the sides of his face, his lips. He sat her gently on the bed and they watched each other un- dress. First his tie, then his shirt, shoes, socks, trousers, and boxers. She pulled her dress up over her head, shedding her mourning garments, her slip, shoes, and stockings.

Robert drew in a deep breath as she stretched out in her black lace bra and panties, her hair fanned out on the pillow. 'Come here, show me just how much you missed me,' she beckoned.

Their kisses intensified. He teased apart her lips, his tongue played with hers. He pushed up against her with his throbbing hardness. He tugged at her panties while kissing her rose-pink nipples through the black lace of the bra. She arched her back to meet him. She had him in her hand and pulled the shaft backward and forward.

Sounds of pleasure spilled from his mouth. Ally pushed him onto his back, his erection tall and alert, ready for her to straddle. Staring directly into his eyes, she impaled herself on the long thick shaft, moaning as his length filled her. Moving up and down his length she squeezed him, urging him deeper. She increased the tempo; his hips rose to meet her.

He grabbed at her buttocks. Robert wanted to slow down, he wanted to stretch out their lovemaking, make it last, but

ALLISON

the passion building in him wouldn't let him. The sight of her moving up and down on top of him, squeezing and releasing him, drove him wild. He grabbed her arse, held her, tried to slow her down, but his heart wasn't in it. 'Ally, I want you to come, I want to feel your shuddering orgasm, then I want to hold you spent in my arms...'

Ally hadn't felt him inside her since that morning at Phuket. Making love now connected them, made her feel alive. The lovers were thrusting harder now. She took him deeper, into her hot slickness. The air smelt of their sex. His cock pulsated and sent wave after wave of juice into her, bringing on her own orgasm. Clenching down on his fading erection, she squeezed out the last drops. Ally cried out as the waves hit her then collapsed onto his chest, her cheek against the dark curly hair covering it. Her lips found his soft and bruised. Silent, they lay for a long time without moving.

'Are you okay, Ally?'

'Yes.' Her breathing was still laboured.

'I love you.' 'I love you too,' Ally said. And she did. This love was different to the love that she had felt for Gavin.

While that love had been real, it had not been the mature love that she felt for Robert. This love healed and hurt her all at the same time, this was the love she had been singing about her whole life.

They spooned naked amongst the tangled sheets. Spent, they slept.

Ally woke to the sound of running water. She called for Robert, but her voice was hoarse, and he didn't hear. She found him in the bathroom, a bubble bath surrounded by candles laid out, fluffy towels on a stool. Andrea Bocelli played softly, and a cool glass of champagne was waiting next to a bowl of strawberries.

'Oh my god,' said Ally. 'It is like something out of the old romance novels my mother used to read.'

Robert was wearing a white towel around his waist. His hair was wet, and he smelt of designer aftershave.

'Oh, you are up.' He smiled.

'I am sorry, was this a private party? You sound so disappointed.'

'I am, because I wanted to wake you, this is for you, so, surprise!' He looked delicious, holding his arms wide in presentation. 'Your bath awaits you, madame.'

She smiled. 'Will you be joining me?'

'I would love to, but I am required elsewhere.'

'Elsewhere? You are leaving? Now?'

'Only as far as the kitchen. Don't worry, my darling, call if you need anything. Dinner will be in forty-five minutes.' He smiled and raised an eyebrow suggestively before leaving her to her bath.

Ally dropped the bed sheet she had been wearing and stepped into the bath, letting the water draw her into its milky, warm luxury. She lay with her head resting on the cool porcelain listening to Bocelli and watching the candlelight play on the ceiling. She wanted to forget about life outside the walls that Robert was surrounding her with, forget what she had lost, and forget that a killer could still be hunting her.

Chapter Fifteen

Robert was clearing the breakfast dishes. He put the dishes on the kitchen bench as the doorbell rang.

'Are we expecting someone?' Ally asked.

'Actually, you are. It is Gavin. I spoke to him at the funeral yesterday and invited him around for coffee. He is worried about you, Ally.'

He opened the door and found Gavin, standing pigeon chested at the threshold. He still loves her, he thought.

'Hello, Gavin,' said Ally. She was skinnier than Gavin remembered her. Dark rings circled her eyes, and she looked drawn and weathered. The two embraced like friends. Gavin was aware that he was being watched closely by her new beau. Even with their history, his place was not in her arms, he had thrown away his place last year. It tore at his heart now when he wanted to be so close to her, to hold her, to be her knight in shining armour. He felt the fool.

'I am just going to get some milk,' said Robert.

'Now?' asked Ally.

Robert nodded, collected his keys, and left the two friends alone.

'He seems nice,' said Gavin.

'Yes, he is nice. How are things between you and Deborah?'

'We broke up just after you left. She wasn't the sharpest tool in the box, and, well, to be honest, it all got dull very quickly. I have missed you. I have missed talking with you.'

'Gavin?'

'I am not here for reconciliation, but I am happy we can still be friends.'

'Me too, I am sorry things did not work out for you two.'

'It is fine, really it is.'

'Gavin, tell me what happened to Renee. We only know what was in the papers.'

'Ally, I can't, because I don't know. The police have not caught him yet, so you need to be careful. No one has a clue where he is. Do the police know that you are back in Perth?'

'No, I should touch base with them.'

'Touch base? Ally, you need protection. Scott might come after you. Don't you think that he might have killed Renee and David to lure you home?'

'Yes, possibly. I will go see the police.' Ally coughed, deep barks that brought blood-soaked phlegm to the tissue she held in front of her mouth.

'Gavin, help me to the bathroom.'

ALLISON

Gavin supported her over the toilet bowl and held back her hair while she hacked up blood and phlegm into the porcelain. 'You should be in hospital.'

'No, no more hospital, just please get my tablets, they are in the kitchen.'

Gavin did as she asked and returned with her medicine and water.

When she was done and the spasm emptied, he carried her to the bedroom, noticing the crumpled sheets over the bed. It was obvious to him that this was not a convalescence bed.

Ally saw the look on his face. 'It is not what you think. I seduced him. Sex is so life affirming, I needed to feel alive. And I love him,' said Ally, falling asleep.

He watched her sleep until he heard the front door opening and closing.

Chapter Sixteen

Robert sat next to Ally on an old wooden bench across from the entry desk. To their left sat an old woman in odd shoes who was mumbling into a handkerchief. Several shopping bags surrounded her feet.

'Are you sure you want to do this today?' he asked.

'I want to get it over with, maybe I can tell them something, maybe they can tell me something? They must capture him. I cannot live my life looking over my shoulder!'

'I understand that, but you should be resting, not at the police station.'

'Robert, a psycho has raped me, stalked me, and killed my best friend. He's on the loose and possibly coming for me, and you want me resting at home where I'm no use to anyone? I need to do something, anything.'

'Of course you do. I'm sorry.' Robert put his arm around her, regretting his timing. He held her to him while the woman at the end of the bench stroked an empty wine bottle she called Whiskers. 'No one will hurt you while I am here.'

'Allison, how are you?' The sergeant appeared at the door.

'Would you like to come this way?'

'Been better,' she whispered and smiled. 'This is Robert, he is my...'

'Partner?' said Robert, turning to the police officer. 'Ally has lost her voice. She has been very ill but has discharged herself early from Southampton General. The funeral, you see...' he added as a way of explanation.

The sergeant nodded.

Ally smiled, happy that even under these circumstances he had referred to her as his partner. Robert took her hand as they followed the sergeant down the wood-grained corridor to a small, windowless room.

'Please.' The sergeant gestured to the chairs surrounding a small, wooden table. 'I am sorry it is a bit dreary, but it is quiet, and we won't be disturbed. I have sent Constable Adams out to fetch some coffees.

'Ally are you sure that you are up to this?' the sergeant asked.

'I am up to doing anything that helps you capture Scott Clarke and make him pay for what he has done to all of us.' Ally forced out the words in a harsh whisper.

'Good. As far as we know, Scott Clarke is not even in Western Australia at this time and he might have no idea that you are here, although...' He stopped as Constable Adams entered the room carrying a cardboard tray with four Dome cappuccinos.

He passed one to each of them and piled sugar bags and paddle pop sticks in the centre of the table. 'It is nice to see you again, Miss Jones. I am sorry it is under such circumstances.'

Yeah, I know what circumstances you would like to meet her under, Robert thought, acutely aware that his feelings for Ally unleashed the green-eyed monster from within, an entirely new experience for him.

'Although what, sergeant?' said Ally, bringing the conversation back on track.

'Although we can't be sure that Scott Clarke is not in town. We really have no way of knowing. The only thing we have to go on is that he has not been seen. His bank accounts have not been accessed, and he has not returned to his last known address in Rockingham since January eighth.'

'The day I left for my cruise?'

'Yes, two days after he escaped police custody,' Adams confirmed.

'Where do we go from here?' asked Robert.

'There is a way to draw him out, but now that I know you are in ill health, I am not sure we should go ahead with it.' The sergeant frowned and looked at Ally, his head cocked.

'Tell me what you want me to do. Tell me how to help you get this arsehole into prison so that I can get on with my life.' Ally strained her voice to be heard.

Robert moved to stand behind Ally, placing his hands on each of her shoulders for support. She reached for his right hand and held it, feeling stronger. 'Please just tell me your plan and let me decide for myself.'

The sergeant took a deep breath before continuing. 'We want you to make a public statement, asking the public to help us find him. We want you to be on everyone's minds, we want you to be interviewed by television, radio and newspaper journalists on the subject of Scott Clarke. We believe that he will come after you, and when he does, we will get him.'

'Excuse me, but that is a ridiculous idea,' said Robert. He stood tall, staring down at the detectives. 'You want Ally to put herself out there for that madman to find her? No way. Ally, you are not doing it. I will take leave, and we will get out of the country. I have relatives in the UK who will look after you until I am permanently discharged. Ally, this is too dangerous.'

'Robert, please, I must do this. I refuse to spend my life looking over my shoulder. It is that simple. If you can't support me in this, I will have to ask you to leave.' Her eyes swelled with tears. The last thing she could bear right now was to have him walk away from her, but she had no other option. If he would not support her, then it would be better if he left. 'Maybe afterwards, we could...' she added meekly.

'Don't be ridiculous. I am not leaving you alone. If you want to do this, then as scared as I am for you, I will be stand by you.' Robert wrapped his arms around her, breathing her in and kissing her softly before taking the seat next to hers.

'That is settled then. I will contact my reporter friend. She works for the Sunday night news. We will arrange the first interview to air on Sunday night. In the meantime, I will set you up with a security detail,' said Sergeant Adams.

Chapter Seventeen

The February sun glared down on the streets of Fremantle, the sea breeze doing little to diminish the heat.

'Maybe today is not a good day for you to be out and about?' said Robert.

'If I listened to you, I would never be out. You heard the doctor yourself. I have had some infection, which seems to have settled down. So now I should work on strengthening myself with light exercise, good food, relaxation, and lots of nice things.' She squeezed the arm that was looped through hers as they walked down South Terrace towards the markets.

'This is hardly relaxation; this is exposure to a psycho.'

'A psycho who has tried to ruin my life and murdered my best friend. I have had enough of Scott Clarke. I can't wait until he is captured by that lovely couple of undercover detectives walking behind us.' She glanced briefly over her shoulder checking that they were still there.

'I don't know about them being a 'lovely couple'. She is holding his hand like he is that stinky kid from primary school no one ever wanted to buddy with.'

'You are so mean, but I see your point. Maybe you could give them some tips on how to be more affectionate?'

They stopped walking and turned to face each other, forcing pedestrian traffic to manoeuvre around them like water around rocks in a stream. The detectives had no choice but to walk past them. Robert's kiss was long and slow. Ally pulled away laughing. Robert squeezed her closer. When they finally released each other, they found that the detectives had looped back and were once again behind them.

The foursome made their way towards the markets, stopping to watch a busker in a purple leotard. He was juggling batons, then knives, and finally chainsaws. The precision of his skill coupled with his ability to chew an apple while juggling impressed the crowds and ensured that his hat was full to the brim by grateful punters.

Ally walked quickly past the fish monger and away from the stench and around to the cottage industry stalls she preferred. A busker was singing near the market pub. An Elkie Brooks song caught Ally in its riff, and the couple parked themselves near an overhead fan and ordered two redback stubbies. The pair sat close to each other, legs and arms touching. Ally listened to the singer's rendition of 'Pearl's a Singer' and wondered when she would be a singer again.

The detectives ordered soft drinks and took a seat at the bar. Detective James Woods was in his tenth year as an undercover detective with the Fremantle Force. His father and his grandfather had been in the force before him. It was what he had wanted to do for as long as he could remember. He had the skills of a chameleon, fitting in with any walk of life. Today he was playing the love interest of the 'cold bitch', or 'CB' as they knew her around the station. Looking at his partner with her shoulder-length, blonde hair, delicate make-up, glossy lips and almond-shaped eyes, James feared that this was to be his toughest assignment yet. She was smiling at their charges sitting a few feet away from them.

'Why are you smiling?' Woods asked her.

'Look.' She gestured to Robert and Ally. Ally's head was resting on Robert's shoulder, his hand softly rubbing her back.

'What? am I looking at?' Woods questioned.

'They are in love, and it is nice. Even though she has a maniac after her, you can see that she still feels safe in his arms.'

'Detective Adams, I never knew you were such a romantic,' he teased.

'There is a lot you don't know about me.' She smiled.

'Is there something you want to tell me?' he asked, an eyebrow raised.

She looked at her new partner. His dark, manicured hair and his penetrating, pale-blue eyes. Amber had first seen him at the station when she was there on work experience with her dad. James had just started. He had looked like a rock star to her, so mature and handsome. She had told the girls at school about the hunk she had met at the station and had even taken her best friend to the station one afternoon under the pretext of seeing her dad so that Jessica could catch a glimpse of him. She smiled. 'You already know everything about me that I want you to know.'

'Look at them.' Ally nudged Robert. 'I bet they would make a great couple.'

'You don't think he's a little old for her? There must be nearly ten years between them.'

'How old is too old? What is age when there is love?'

'What is anything when there is love?' He kissed her forehead.

They listened to the singer belt out a rendition of 'Hit the Road Jack' while watching shoppers passed by. A figure in a black overcoat drew Woods' attention. He watched the figure walk past Ally and Robert as they were enjoying their beer and nachos, like any regular couple out on a Sunday in Fremantle.

'Look at the man in the black overcoat,' Woods said to Amber. 'It is thirty-five degrees outside. Keep your eye on him. I will get these guys back to the station until we hear from you.'

Amber nodded and set off to follow her detail. He was ambling through the crowded alleyways of the markets, past the honey seller and into the part of the market selling fresh produce.

'Can you smell that? Smoke.' Robert sniffed the air like a hunting dog and turned to Woods, who gestured that it was time to go. They stood as the deafening ring from the fire alarms alerted the crowd to danger. Chaos. Shoppers ran for the exits, sellers packed up their money and personnel items, leaving their stock where it lay. Shutters thudded down. Panic. Smoke filled the air.

Crouching low to escape the dense smoke, Ally, Robert, and Woods joined the crowd pushing towards the exit and out onto Adelaide Terrace. Fire trucks screamed into place to attack the blaze. Ambulances helped the asphyxiated. Woods searched the crowd for his partner while an ambulance officer attended to Ally, who was now coughing and vomiting from the effects of the smoke on her throat.

'You need to be admitted to hospital,' the ambulance officer said.

Unable to talk, her voice hoarse from the heat and the smoke, Ally shook her head, wincing from the movement before she collapsed into Robert's arms.

'Well, that is settled then,' said Robert.

Woods returned carrying his partner in his arms. Blood flowed from a gash on her forehead.

'What happened?' Robert was lifting Ally onto the ambulance gurney the ambulance officer indicated.

'I am not sure. She is not making much sense. She mumbled something about Clarke. I found her near the apple seller,' said Woods.

Woods was guided to another ambulance and introduced himself and the semi-lucid Amber. The ambulance officer introducing himself as, 'Drew, a Sagittarius and not afraid to date a woman in uniform,' gestured for Woods to put her on the gurney, and he began to take her vitals.

'I take it that you are frowning from your pain, and not in rejection of my advances,' Drew said in faux scolding.

'It is hardly an appropriate way to talk to an officer in or out of uniform, is it?' Amber answered.

'Yes, but it keeps you talking, and you are easier to treat if you can talk.' He smiled. 'Don't worry, you are not my type, your partner is more up my alley.' He winked, and Amber laughed at the thought of Detective Woods on a date with Drew. She took another breath of Penthrox from the green stick.

Amongst the smell of burnt plastic and future landfill was the smell of roasted nuts and meats from the delis, burnt bread, and a hint of essential oils. An eclectic mix of all that the market offered the weekend stroller, a palette of the necessary, the useless and the wanted. Pedestrians were pushed along by the police, scanning the crowd for Scott Clarke. It would be hours before traffic could move through South Terrace again with the rubberneckers slowing the flow.

Robert sat in the vinyl chair next to Ally's bed, watching a live report showing images of the smouldering remains. A drip-fed fluids and Malaxon into Ally's veins while an oxygen mask worked to clear the smoke from her scarred airways. Ally lay in the hospital bed.

She was beautiful and fragile. He would kill Scott Clarke if he ever had the opportunity. After the sun set and the city lights flickered to life, the doctor returned with Ally's results. She was still asleep. The doctor gestured for Robert to join him near the door. In a low voice he explained.

'Despite her previous treatment, Miss Jones is still testing positive for strep, so we will give her some IV antibiotics. I think that if she rests properly this time and is kept relatively stress free, then she should be back to her old self in a week or so.' He smiled reassuringly at Robert.

'Just one question, doctor,' Robert said. 'Ally is a singer; do you think her voice will recover?'

'I cannot see any reason she wouldn't be able to sing again. However, I can refer her to a throat specialist if there is a residual problem. Let her get over the infection first, then we'll see.'

Robert sat on in the darkened room and held her hand. The bustling, chaotic sounds of an excited Fremantle rose from the streets to the top floor ward of the hospital.

'Ally, I wonder if you can hear me. The doctor said that you will be fine. You just need to rest. I love you, Ally. I will be here when you wake up, I promise.' His soft, soothing voice cut through the darkness. He kissed her hand and then, slumped over the foot of her bed, he slept.

Chapter Eighteen

Downstairs in the casualty department, Amber was having the last of twenty-eight stitches applied to her wound. Emerging from the cubicle with a large white gauze bandage around her head, she found Wood attaching a wanted notice to the emergency room pin-up board. Amber stopped next to him. The analgesics the doctor had administered were making her a little un- steady on her feet.

'Whoa, cowboy.' Woods took her by the arm to prevent her from falling face first onto the corkboard in front of them.

'He is not a bad-looking guy. It's a shame he is such a psycho.' She pointed to the picture of Scott Clarke.

'Shit, you are a mess. Come on, let's get you home,' said Woods, amused.

'Do not think that you can take advantage of me,' she slurred. 'I don't have a crush on you anymore. I am all grown up!'

'A crush you say. And when did you have this crush on me?' Woods laughed.

'Shush, I am not going to tell you that it was when I did work experience years ago at the station, you didn't even know I was alive,' Amber whispered.

'Hang on, is your dad Sergeant Adams? The man who took down those bank robbers and, the one who found that little boy in the national forest down south? Didn't he get some award?'

'He sure did. Then he got something else, 'A World's Greatest Dad' mug from me.'

Woods loaded Amber into his car. So that explained the chip on her shoulder. Why she had to be so perfect all the time. Even before they had been assigned to each other, he had known that she was a pedantic pain in the arse. He had also followed his father into the force, but he wasn't trying to live up to the old man's name. His father had died in a motorcycle chase the same day that Adams had found that young boy in the national park down south. Woods father had received an award for his service on that day too.

'Where do you live, Amber?' She was slumped in the passenger seat of his Falcon.

'On Rankin Street near the docks, over the bridge.' She pointed vaguely through the windscreen.

'Just around the corner from me. Who knew?'

'Stalker!' She laughed, then fell asleep before the car rolled onto South Terrace.

Ally tossed and turned haunted by the nightmares brought on by another high fever. The nurses were at a loss to explain it. They called in the doctor for more tests and administered paracetamol for the fever along with regular tepid sponge bathing. Robert soothed Ally's forehead and pulse points with a cool flannel while the nurse sponged her torso and legs. Robert tried not to stare. He could feel himself becoming semi-hard and for a moment he hated his maleness.

Later, he excused himself and went home to shower and change out of his smoke infested clothes. He returned to her side within an hour. Her temperature was still at forty-one degrees.

Chapter Nineteen

'Welcome back to the land of the living.' said Woods, 'How is the head?'

'Massive headache! Did they give me anything at the hospital last night? And why are you here?' Amber winced at the sun shining through her French doors.

'I need some Panadol and coffee.' On the way to the kitchen, Amber passed Woods on the couch where he had spent the night.

'Have you been here all night?'

'No, I spent some of the night on that very uncomfortable designer chair in your bedroom watching you sleep. I had to wake you up every hour to make sure that you were okay. I eventually came out here to make myself a sandwich and help myself to a beer or three. I didn't think that you would mind. The captain has called to check on you, by the way,' said Woods.

ALLISON

'You mean the captain knows that you spent the night with me?' said Amber.

'Calm down, I didn't spend the night with you in a romantic sense, did I? I don't think the captain thinks I could make you switch teams, even if you did once have a crush on me.' Woods grinned at her.

'Well, you can leave any time, you know.' Amber changed the filter in the percolator, added coffee, and switched the dripping water on. The hiss of the steam and the fragrance of fresh coffee woke her senses.

Switch teams! No one ever asked me what team I was on. They just assumed, and because I have never corrected them... well at least it stopped the guys from the station from hitting on me; the odd joke or lewd comment I can handle, having my heart broken again, no, thank you.

Despite her anger at Woods, she handed him another coffee. 'Any leads on the case?' she asked.

'Nothing. The man has eluded us again. The market is a write-off. The fire started in the storage room behind the bakery. It will be a while before it is up and running again. But you don't have to worry about any of that anymore, you are off the case now. I am sorry, kid.'

'Kid? Off the case? How is that fair? I want to get that bastard as much as you do!'

'You are injured, and you know that it is against regulations to work with an injury. You need to take some time off.'

Amber sighed as she sat heavily onto the couch opposite him. 'Well, at least let me go to the station and go over the files on the case. Come on, I will go stir crazy here. I might even find something.'

Woods admired her tenacity. 'I suppose there's no point saying no. You'll probably turn up and do it anyway, but you're in no condition to drive, so I'll give you a lift in when you are ready.'

On the way to the station, Woods slowed the car down as they drove past the charred remains of Fremantle Markets. Fire investigators were still picking their way through the debris, putting out the odd spot fire that could easily reignite on the hot Fremantle day.

Soot and ash had infiltrated all the surrounding homes and businesses within a five-kilometre radius. The window of Ally's hospital room was grey with soot. Robert gazed out at the scene below, people going about their business, ignorant to the fact that a killer was on the loose. He had his own plan. He could no longer depend on the police to protect the woman he loved.

On Tuesday, Ally's fever calmed. She slept peacefully, muttering the odd word under her breath to keep his attention. For the third night, Robert slept slumped over the foot of her bed exhausted. He awoke to Ally's foot moving underneath him.

'Robert.'

He moved towards her, bleary eyed. 'Ally, you are awake! Thank the gods, all of them.' He smiled, framing her pale face with his hands and showering her with kisses.

'Can I have a drink of water?' she whispered hoarsely.

She gulped at the cup of water he poured from the jug on her bedside table.

'Slow down, you have had nothing to drink for days. These tubes have been keeping you alive.'

'It is just the smoke; I can taste it in my mouth. How long have I been here?'

ALLISON

'This is your third night. The doctors have done all the tests again and think exhaustion is the major problem along with Dr Patel's strep diagnosis. I am glad to have you back. Ally, I have been thinking, my grandfather has a fishing cabin in Albany. We should go there until they catch Clarke. What do you think? It is miles away from anywhere; I can keep you safe there, I promise. You need to rest. Playing bait for a psycho is too much for you now.' Robert's eyes searched her face.

She shook her head. 'The police are convinced that he will come after me. I must do this before he hurts someone else.'

Her voice was fading with the strain of emotions that she could not communicate. He nodded and sat down next to her, taking her into his arms. 'As you wish. Just promise me that I am not going to lose you.'

Later that day, Woods came to visit Ally. While she dozed, Robert told him of his plan to get Ally away.

'I am not going,' Ally whispered, her eyes half open.

'You should definitely go.' Woods was standing at the foot of her hospital bed. 'Scott Clarke is more dangerous than we expected. This man has followed you to the United Kingdom. We found his digs at the back of your old house in South Perth, can you believe it?' Woods spread a file out on her table. There were photos of her singing on the ship, of Robert and her in Nagasaki. 'He has been with you the whole time.'

'But I read that he escaped to Queensland. How did he get on the ship?' Robert shifted to Ally's side.

'We stopped for a day in Brisbane,' whispered Ally. 'Why would he do that?'

'It is a common practice in serial killers to play a cat- and-mouse game with their victims. Scott Clarke is an increasingly dangerous threat. He is becoming more and more violent with every attack. We need to get you to somewhere safe while having him think that you are still here. This man appears to have resources we had never even considered. I am sorry, Ally, but your life is in danger, and you will not be safe until we catch him,' said Woods.

'As soon as you are fit to travel, I am taking you to Albany,' said Robert.

'Where will you be in Albany?' asked Woods.

'My grandfather has a fishing cabin down there: it is isolated, secure, and you can see for miles around.'

'Good, let me know the exact address, and I will get a detail down there to set up surveillance equipment and secure the location. I won't be notifying the local police, but I will organise a specialised security detail from Perth to stay with you. I can guarantee they have no connection with Scott Clarke, and they are lethal when provoked.'

'Good, that's settled then. I will get the doctor and see when we can leave.' Robert kissed the hand he was holding and smiled. 'You will be okay, Ally.'

When he left the room, she was alone with Woods. 'Will I really be okay, detective?' she whispered.

Three days in the affectionately named 'shack' was enough to make Ally feel like her old self again. The very luxurious, one-bedroom cabin was fully equipped with a gourmet kitchen, spa bathroom, lap pool, and all-round balcony with breathtaking panoramic views of the ocean and boulder cliffs. Two guards camped at the rear of the cabin on the only road that accessed their retreat.

ALLISON

'This place is amazing!' Ally said to Robert over a breakfast feast of croissants, fresh fruit, and brewed coffee. 'I could truly get use to this kind of lifestyle. What did your grandfather do?'

'Not sure. He was with The Australian Security Intelligence Organisation (ASIO), that is all we knew. This place was never a family retreat as such, just somewhere for him and Nan to go. The first time I was invited up here was after she passed away. I don't think he enjoyed being up here so much on his own. Together we would fish, sometimes he would disappear on long walks by himself and come back energised. He would often say that Eileen was on the beach. Eileen was my grandmother. Then he would cook the most amazing meals. This kitchen has every gadget known to man, from apple corers to zesters!'

'He must have thought a lot of you, to bring you here.'

'I suppose. We always got on well. I was not very popular with the cousins when he left this place to me. But he knew I wouldn't just sell it for a quick buck.'

'He knew that you would respect this place and what it meant to him and your nan.'

'Yes, I understood him. He was a sentimental man, because of his work, I think. He saw so many terrible things that he cherished the small things that many others only take for granted.'

'This, for example.' Ally gestured to their breakfast of fresh croissants, fruit, market jam, and brewed coffee.

'Yes, and the pleasure of waking to hearing the woman you love breathing next to you. Listening to the soft rhythms of her sleep and, oh, copping a feel under her nighty before she wakes up.'

He laughed and caught the strawberry she tossed at him. He leaned around the table and pulled Ally's chair to his. He kissed her, tasting the jam on her tongue. They explored the well-trodden territory of each other's mouths.

Ally slid her arms around his neck, and a long leg slid across his lap. She shuffled herself forward until she was seated firmly on his lap, straddling him with both feet on the floor.

His hand crept into the small space between them, under her nightie to her naked skin where it found her tender breast.

He rolled the hardness of her nipple between his thumb and finger, and she threw her head back with a long, deep moan of pleasure. Her wetness seeped through his silk pyjama bottoms, outlining the hardness of him.

She found the button on the fly of his pants and set his erect cock free. Swiftly she manoeuvred her hips to impale herself on his thick, hard shaft. Building the rhythm slowly, Ally showered kisses along the nape of his neck, from behind his ear to his shoulder. He held onto her breast, enjoying the feel of warm wetness gripping his cock, drawing him deeper inside her.

As a backdrop to the lovers was the panoramic views of King George Sound, twenty-metre-high boulders and the steep descent to the shoreline.

'Fucking paradise!' Ally bit Robert's lip as she took in the view. His hard body rocked beneath her, urging her to draw him in deeper. She resisted the urge to come, wanting to make love slowly. His beautiful cock was the perfect fit, caressing her g-spot with ease. Making love to Robert was an easy pleasure. From her vantage point, she saw the waves crashing against the rocks below. Her hands gripped his hair as he brought her to a white-hot, shuddering climax. Her contracting muscles drew him deeper inside her, making it difficult for him to hold his own.

Robert shifted his focus to his own pelvic floor and climaxed without coming on the ripple of her pleasure.

In one move, he was on his feet, carrying Ally. She wrapped her legs around him as he carried her out to the balcony and leaned her against the teak banister. She clung to him, taking him deep inside of her. Thrusting, his mouth on her left breast, biting down on the erect nipple. A warm breeze caressed over them, the sun warm on her naked back, an earlobe between her teeth.

He carried her to the outdoor chaise lounge and laid her down, towering above her. He took in her curvaceous, soft body laid out before him. Full, rounded breasts with pink, rosebud nipples. The gentle curve of her waist and the smooth mound of her stomach were soft and womanly. His attention rested on the brown, velvet, carpeted triangle of her womanhood, showing just a glimpse of wet, pink flesh. Robert knelt at the foot of the lounge and pushed his hands under her buttocks, raising her to meet his mouth.

Sounds of pleasure escaped her even before his tongue met her clitoris. She opened wide for him. A hint of breeze caressed over her as she watched him watching her over her mound. He gorged himself on her juices, her sex.

Robert took pleasure in the taste of Ally: sweet, salty, sexy. His tongue ambled through her folds, and he watched her watch him until pleasure overtook her. He inserted two fingers inside of her and moved them rhythmically in time with his tongue. When she was close to climaxing, he moved his fingers more deliberately and ignited her clitoris with his tongue moving across the width of it until the pleasure took her away, on wave after wave of glorious ecstasy. Hot ambrosia melted from inside her and fed her lover.

He suckled deeply on his reward before pushing his erection home, deep inside the swells of her wet, welcoming sex. Their steady pace sped to a frenzy of thrusting. She came as another wave of heat shuddered throughout her body from the tips of her toes up to her arching back and rolling eyes. He stopped, exploding his load into her.

She drew him in until he was deliciously spent. He collapsed onto her, giving into exhaustion and bliss.

A puddle of sweat suctioned their bellies together and they remain there. Joined. A single entity out in the open breeze. The soft ocean breeze cooled their sweat beaded skin.

A dinner tray lay untouched at the foot of his hospital bed. Gavin was still too tired from the emergency surgery to bother with food. The smell had been enough to make him nauseous as he drifted back to sleep. Deborah sat at his bedside reading the latest issue of Cosmo and munching on a crunchie. She sipped the Diet Coke she had bought from the hospital gift shop on the way up. He did not even know that she was there, and she knew she shouldn't be. They had not seen each other since Ally returned for the funeral. It was Ally he asked for when he had woken briefly, so she had called the contact number he had in his wallet and talked to Detective Woods, who promised to pass the message on.

'Ally.' The name was bitter on Deborah's lips. Ally had caused all this trouble, getting involved with a maniac, and now 'poor Ally' was all that anyone cared about. What about poor Deborah, who had watched Gavin from afar for a whole year before getting up the courage to move in on him? What about poor Deborah, who had the name Ally whispered into her ear when the man she loved was making love to her on a boozy night? Ally.

Cosmo advertised 'Ten Ways to Drive Him Wild'. Deborah wondered why they didn't write 'Ten Ways to Help Him Remember that You Exist'. She felt a fool.

Regardless of everything that he had said to her, he was still not over Ally. Even with her out of the way, Gavin still found it hard to connect with Deborah on anything more than a physical level. What did Ally have that Deborah didn't?

Gavin woke again to the familiar smell of Deborah's perfume, but when he opened his eyes, he was alone with just a tray of half-eaten sandwiches and a bowl of red jelly.

'Ally, you cannot go back to Perth, it is too dangerous!' Robert pleaded.

'He is right, Ally. Leaving now would expose you again, and you really have not had enough time to regain your strength,' Detective Woods agreed.

'Look, I am going. I do not care if I have to go in disguise. You can have guards follow me, no one will even know that it is me,' said Ally.

'This is what Clarke wants. He is trying to lure you out of hiding by attacking the people he knows you care about,' said Robert.

'I know, but he was there for me. Now I must do the same for him. It is my fault he is in this situation.'

'Ally, there is no one to blame but Scott Clarke. What about Deborah, can't she help Gavin? She phoned Woods, after all,' said Robert.

'The last time I spoke to Gavin, he said they had broken up. How can you two expect me to stay here and do nothing? Gavin is family to me, and you want me to do nothing!' Her voice was hoarse.

'Ally just call him and see what he wants you to do,' Robert suggested, guessing that Gavin would not encourage Ally to put herself in danger.

'A voice of reason. Ring him,' Woods encouraged Ally.

'Okay, I will do that now.' Ally agreed and walked into the bedroom, closing the door behind her.

He answered on the ring. 'Hello, Gavin, it is me, Ally.' She sat on the bed holding the mouthpiece with both hands.

'Ally, it is nice to hear your voice. You sound more like your old self.'

'I am feeling better, but you sound tired. How are you doing?'

'The surgery went well. The doctor says I will be out of here by the end of the week.'

'Surgery? What for?'

'No one told you?'

'No one knows. Woods just knows that you are in hospital.'

'The police here think that it was a simple home burglary. A man was there when I arrived home, going through cupboards. He had smashed the TV and computer, upturned the furniture. Your stuff was opened and turned out; you know the boxes stored at my place?'

She nodded pointlessly. 'Gavin, was it him?'

'I don't know. I couldn't identify him. He was wearing a balaclava and a ninja costume when I saw him going through your things, I said, "Hey, what the fuck are you doing?" He turned and he pushed past me in the hallway, and he stabbed me with our master chef knife. I turned to chase him but then collapsed. Blood was spurting out, and I thought I was going to die. Then and there. Luckily, Peter from across the street was taking his bins out and saw the ninja run from the house. He saved my life, Ally.'

'Thank god for Peter. The police tell me that I can't come back to see you. They say it is too dangerous but, I am afraid something might happen to you.'

'Ally, I am leaving Perth for a while. I will stay with my sister in Christchurch. Hayley is arranging everything from her end. I fly out on Saturday. If I could be of any help to you, I would stay, Ally, you know that, but you have all the help you need.'

'Gavin, when this is over, I will call you.' Ally realised then that she would not be calling Gavin at all. It was time to say goodbye to her first love for good. When Ally returned to the living room and plopped herself down on the lounge, the two men stopped talking. She reached for a copy of National Geographic off the glass coffee table.

'Well?' Robert was the first to speak.

'You were right, he doesn't want me to go to Perth. In fact, he is leaving for New Zealand at the weekend. His sister has arranged everything.'

'You sound disappointed,' said Robert. *She is hiding something.*

He thinks.

'I am disappointed. Things may be over between me and Gavin, but he is also someone else that Scott Clarke has taken away from me in one way or another. It seems your biggest problem isn't keeping me safe, Detective, it is keeping the people around me safe.' Returning the magazine to the table, she got up to get herself a drink from the Marri bar. 'Care to join me?' she asked the pair.

'I really shouldn't. I have to drive back to Albany for the night,' said Woods.

'I can make up the spare bed. Your trip from Perth must have tired you. Why not stay and have dinner?' Ally asked. 'Robert caught some Taylor this morning we were just going to throw it on the barbeque.' Ally looked at Robert, who nodded slowly.

Woods accepted their invitation. *It would be nice to have some company on my birthday for a change.*

'Anything I can do to help?' he offered, following Ally to the kitchen.

Robert felt the odd man out. He wanted to know what had happened with Gavin. He couldn't understand why Ally had invited the detective for dinner, when they should have been alone discussing her feelings or making love. Suddenly he was afraid that something had changed between them. Robert's leave was running out, and he didn't know what would happen to their relationship when he was called away on duty for months at a time. He watched Ally peeling potatoes, talking and laughing in the kitchen with Woods, and he wondered if she was avoiding him deliberately.

When Woods excused himself to go the bathroom, Ally whispered that Amber had called after she had hung up with Gavin to tell her that it was Woods's birthday. 'We couldn't let him stay in that run-down hotel on his birthday,' she said.

Robert, relieved, kissed her.

After a meal of barbecued fish, green salad, and baby potatoes, Robert opened another bottle of Wolf Blass Chardonnay. The three new friends sat on the balcony overlooking Betty's Beach.

ALLISON

In the darkness, the surf crashed onto the shore. Clouds gathered overhead, greyness covered the black, and a lightning show replaced the stars. Ally and her two guards watched the show in companionable silence.

Ally drained the last drop of chardonnay from the bottle as the sky burst open and dumped summer rain on the diners. The dishes were left exposed to the elements as they raced inside with a wineglass in hand to settle on the couch and watch the storm over the ocean through the floor to ceiling window.

There was a knock on the door. Woods sprang to attention, regretting the wine he had drunk at dinner. 'Get into the kitchen and stay out of sight,' he ordered Ally and Robert. Slowly he opened the door with his gun in hand.

'What the hell are you doing here?'

'You are pissed! That is why I am here. How are you going to protect anyone?' Amber poked his chest playfully.

'How are you going to protect anyone with twenty- eight stitches in your head?'

'I will scare them with my Herman Munster routine. Happy birthday, Woods.' Amber kissed him on the cheek, pulling his head close, with her hand in his hair. She held him there for longer than was necessary.

Woods blushed. 'How did you know it was my birthday?' he asked, heat coursing through him.

'It is my job to know everything about my partner. Are you at least going to invite me in? I have some important information for you.'

'Sorry.' He moved away from the door and watched her walk past in her short, cheesecloth dress. Her legs were shapely, womanly, and golden. The kiss still burned on his cheek.

Joining Robert and Amber in the lounge, he sat across from her, his back to the window. 'You are missing the show.' Amber gestured to the lightning charging up the darkness.

'You had something to tell me,' he said, returning their talk deliberately to business in an attempt to take his mind off her long legs, the valley of her cleavage, and the curls framing her face. Somehow, his frigid partner had become a woman.

Ally appeared at the kitchen door holding a cake alive with candles just as the power cut out.

'Nice timing,' said Robert. Ally broke into a beautiful rendition of the birthday song before putting the cake on the table in front of Woods; he blushed in the candlelight, unsure of what to do. Embarrassed by the attention, he looked at Amber and narrowed his eyes. 'Big mouth!'

'Blow out the candles before you start a house fire,' she said, smiling across the flames at him.

'Don't forget to make a wish,' said Ally.

Closing his eyes, Woods blew out all thirty-six candles and wished for the courage to ask Amber out and for Scott Clarke to be captured.

'Thank you,' he said, 'but you really shouldn't have gone to all this trouble.'

'Of course, we should have! After all that you are doing for us,' said Ally, lifting the cake. She went back to the kitchen and returned with four coffees and four slices of cake while Robert brought the house alive with lighted candles. Flickering shadows danced on the surrounding walls. The chocolate tiramisu cake from Albany's baker was thick and rich, creamy and soft.

'I have not had a birthday cake since my mum passed away on my twenty-first.'

ALLISON

'On your twenty-first?' asked Amber. 'That must have been hard for you. I am sorry for your loss.'

'I am sorry too. I know how hard it is to lose your mother. You must still miss her?' asked Ally.

'Actually, I don't. We weren't close,' Woods said.

'How about a movie?' said Robert, trying to lighten the mood.

'Good idea, but there is no power,' said Ally.

'Ah, she of little faith, there is a generator,' said Robert.

'Why didn't you just put it on when the power went out?'

'Because I like candles. They are romantic, don't you think?' He smiled and kissed her.

'I'll give you a hand.' Woods rose from his seat and followed Robert. While Ally hunted out a movie, Amber sat watching the lightning show. She realised that there was so much more to Woods than what she had ever imagined. She wanted to get close to him, to touch him again.

Ally found a copy of Message in a Bottle. 'Do you think the boys will go for it?'

'Who cares, I love that movie!'

'You will stay the night, won't you Amber?' said Ally. 'I would like to stay if you have the room.'

'I am afraid we only have one room, but that room enters the kitchen and bathroom from the other side, so I can guarantee you won't be disturbed.'

'Where is Woods sleeping?'

'Out here. There are two couches.'

'Perfect.' Amber smiled. 'Any more wine? I may require some Dutch courage later.'

Laughing, Ally gestured to the kitchen and followed Amber to fetch a cheese board for them to snack on.

Robert and Woods returned to find the girls facing the large TV ready for the movie.

'Amber, you came here to tell me something about the case, what was it?' Woods asked.

'The attack on Gavin was not done by Scott Clarke. Forensics found hair matching that of Deborah Zabriskie's in a balaclava like the one Gavin described, in a bin behind the shops near his house. It seems she dumped the evidence there. They have arrested her, and they have found the knife with her fingerprints and Gavin's blood on it too. Her lawyer has petitioned for a psychological assessment.'

As the previews ran, Ally snuggled into the crook of Robert's arm. He held her tight to him, worried about the danger she was still in. Finding Gavin's attacker had solved nothing. Scott Clarke was still at large.

At some time during the movie Ally and Robert retired to their bedroom, leaving Amber and Woods alone sleeping on the couch together, leaning up against one another for support in the darkness. Outside the storm raged, the wind howled, and lightening lit the sky, chased by roaring thunder.

When Amber woke, she was in Woods's arms. It was a warm place to be. 'Woods,' she whispered. She breathed in the smell of him, drawing him into her body. She reached up to touch his cheek. A light beard tickled her hand; soft, downy, not what she had expected. She ran a finger over his lips. His very kissable, full lips, soft and pink. She didn't want to wake him, but she wanted him to kiss her, now. Sitting up slightly, she turned to face him and lightly kissed his lips. She felt his arm draw around her and pull her closer into him.

ALLISON

He woke to his mouth being teased. He could smell her on him, and he wanted to pull himself inside of her. Her lips opened slightly over his, his tongue flickered in and out of her mouth, exploring the possibilities. His head was reeling with the realisation that he was not dreaming. He could taste her, a faint hint of wine flavoured her warm, wet, mouth. They kissed deeper.

Woods's hand found her breast. Her nipples hardened through the cotton of her dress. Pulling a strap down, he ex- posed her. He drew in a deep breath at her beauty, the shape of her. The sight swelled him against the fly of his jeans. He took her nipple in his mouth, bit down with hunger. She tasted sweet.

He removed the other strap, and her white cotton dress fell to her waist. He grabbed her breasts, one in each hand, squeezing them as she moved to straddle him. He shifted slightly, releasing a groan as she sat directly on his aching cock, mere fabric separating him from her. Amber rocked her hips back and forth, making his erection shift hard against the fabric of his jeans. Her panties were wet in anticipation of him. He teased her nipple with his tongue, then he bit down hard.

A shudder of pain, immediately followed by pleasure, wet her more. She ran her hands through his lustrous hair and kissed his forehead. Reaching her hands to either side of his face, she pulled up his head and kissed him deeply. His bulge rose beneath her, and she could wait no longer. Standing in front of him, she let her dress and panties fall to the floor. He watched her as she stepped out of them and was surprised when she kneeled before him to undo his jeans. She smiled up at him, her sexy eyes fixed on his as she reached into his Calvin's and freed his pulsating cock. She caressed slowly, up and down. Flames of want ran through him. Fear that she would stop nagged at him; the scene was dreamlike.

Amber licked and then rolled her tongue around his delicious head before sucking him. Her hand worked the length of his thick cock while her mouth teased him to abandon. Woods resisted the urge to buck his hips and force his cock deep inside her mouth. He wanted to feel her all along the size of him. His cock throbbed for more, he ached. It was heaven and hell at the moment. She worked his cock, bringing him to the edge, and then pushed against his perineum to stop the stream of cum spilling into her mouth.

She let him go. The respite relieved him.

Woods was eager to return the favour. 'Fair is fair.' he whispered, standing up to kick his own pants away. He pulled her to her feet and shuddered as her hand skimmed his cock. The length of him pushed into her taut stomach as he pulled her close and, he kissed her softly. 'Take a seat.'

She obeyed his request. He opened her legs, revealing her shining wetness in the dim light, guiding his way. She moaned at the anticipation of him touching her. His hands caressed her thighs, and as she had done, he kneeled before her. Drawing in her scent, he gently tongued her soft woman lips apart, first the outer labia then the welcoming minor. Sounds of pleasure escaped Amber's mouth. She squeezed at her own breasts, and he ached at the sight of her spread before him. His tongue flickered and teased her lips, sending her wild. He gently inserted a finger inside of her, feeling her, making her want his cock more. She raised her hips towards him as he moved inside her. He took her clitoris between his teeth, gently nibbling and sucking. As she came in waves, he was unable to wait any longer. He plunged his hard, thick cock inside of her. She was gone, riding the waves of her first orgasm. He kissed her neck, her hips moved in time with his thrusting, working towards his own sweet release. Amber's hands follow the muscular hard curves of his body, her mouth sucked his nipple sending him over the edge. His juices flowed into her, and the musty smell of sex filled the air.

They turned their bodies to face each other, her legs wrapped around him. Woods pulled her close, wanting desperately to stay inside of her. 'This is a dream, isn't it?' he whispered. 'This is too good to be true.' He kissed her.

She bit down hard on his bottom lip, and he recoiled at the shock of it. 'When you wake up, that will remind you that this was not a dream. You just fucked the captain's daughter.'

'The captain's alleged lesbian daughter?'

'That's right. Now that was either just a rumour, or you just made me change teams.' Smiling, she reached for the blanket Ally had left out for them. She felt him go limp inside her just before sleep took her. They slept together tight through the night.

'Ally! What are you doing?' Robert was woken by the sound of the rain pounding on the steel roof. He searched the darkness for Ally, and he found her on the balcony barely sheltered by the eaves from the rain.

'I can't sleep,' she said, smiling at him. Unable to sleep, she had walked into the living area and caught sight of Woods and Amber fucking on his grandfather's leather couch. The vision had mesmerised her. Not wanting to disturb them, she had snuck out through the open balcony door and crouched there, watching them. She couldn't help herself; they were beautiful. It wasn't simple sex; it was the joining of two hungry souls. Watching them had made her wet, and she wanted Robert. Now! She kissed him. 'Let's go to bed; I want you to make love to me,' she said.

Chapter Twenty

The entwined naked couple woke to a crash. Woods and Amber were dressed and radioing down to the guards on the road before Ally and Robert entered the lounge. 'What was that?' Woods shouted into the walkie talkie while checking his gun. Robert wrapped a protective arm around Ally.

'There is a fire coming up the hill. It is starting to get out of control, and police are recommending that residents who are not prepared to bunker down and defend their properties evacuate the area,' said the voice on the radio.

'Okay,' Woods replied. 'You blokes head back to town while the road is clear. We will be right behind you. How long before they close the road?'

'A couple of hours,' said the voice.

'What was that bang we heard?'

ALLISON

'Looks like a tree on the east side of the house fell down. It happens down here during storms. Roots weak as piss on some of them. Catch you back in town,' said the voice.

'Do we have time for breakfast?' said Ally, making her way through to the kitchen.

'Yes,' said Robert. 'I need some food too.'

The summer morning heat had already dried the arid bush land, creating ample fuel for the fire. Six fire trucks from the surrounding districts were already on it, but a blaze such as this could spell disaster if the hot winds kept blowing. It could destroy the surrounding farmlands in hours, swallowing everything in its wake. From their vantage point they could see the flames in the distance and the black smoke rising as the fire ate up acres upon acres of natural bushland.

After a quick breakfast of toast and coffee, the two couples packed their cars and prepared to leave.

'Stay close. Fires can turn on a dime here.' Woods climbed into his car, lifting his eyes to the blackening sky.

Robert tried to start his car without success, then Amber tried hers and nothing. Neither motor would turn over.

'I don't like the look of this.' Woods popped the hood to Amber's car. Both the distributor leads were missing. 'Someone has been fucking around with the motor; this thing isn't going anywhere.'

Closer inspection of the other cars revealed the same problem. They were trapped on the cliff side of Betty's Beach with a fire closing in all around them.

'What are we going to do?' Ally asked. 'We can't stay here.'

'We must, we can't risk leaving on foot if the fire turns and we get trapped. We will have no chance,' said Amber.

'If we prepare the house, we can stay to defend it. My grandfather made sure the house was well equipped for such emergencies. We will be okay,' said Robert.

'Let's not forget Clarke. I will telephone the station and let them know what has happened. I will request that they send us help as soon as possible.' Woods walked back to the house with Amber.

'Woods,' said Amber, 'about last night...' I want to do it again, she wanted to say, but he interrupted her.

'Have dinner with me when this is all over?'

'Sure,' she said, 'I would like that.' Smiling despite their situation, Amber joined Ally and Robert in the kitchen.

'Okay,' said Woods, walking into the room, 'they will try to a get a chopper out to us from Albany, but the conditions are bad, so we will have to bunker down and wait.'

The sky grew darker with smoke and ash. The fire front moved towards them. Water bomber planes dump their loads in an effort to extinguish the fire, and flames hissed as steam rose from the scorched earth. The bombers succeeded in temporarily narrowing the path of the fire, only to have it expand again once the winds changed.

The foursome bunkered down in the house; outside the sprinklers wet the roof and surrounds, the outside shutters were drawn, so only a light in the kitchen from the skylight cast a dull hue over the room. Smoke seeped in as the fire raged around them. Robert kept watch in the ceiling cavity for stray embers. Woods checked and re-fitted wet cloth seals on the external doors.

Ally and Amber sat in the kitchen watching as the blackness outside shrouded them in smoky darkness. The house was silent but for the crackling outside, then the thunderous roar of flames passing. It took only minutes for it to consume its fill of dry fuel around the house and continued blowing up the coast.

Amber turned to see Ally crying. 'Ally are you all right?'

Ally shook her head.

'Robert, come over here. Ally needs you,' said Amber as Ally hit the floor.

She was unconscious, shaking uncontrollably. Robert turned her on her side.

'She is having a seizure,' said Amber. 'I'll get something to stop her biting her tongue.' She disappeared into the kitchen and returned with a wooden spoon. Ally was sweat-soaked and shaking helplessly on the floor.

Robert steadied her head, and Amber called the triple zero. 'What do you mean you are unable to get us help?' Her voice rose a pitch. 'I know the roads are closed. What about a helicopter? Fine, what can we do?' She listened carefully to the instructions and ended the call. She put down the phone, sat heavy on the sofa where Ally was convulsing at her feet. Pooled in sweat and piss when she lost her capacity.

'They can't help us right now, but we need to give her aspirin, is she epileptic?' Amber stood up and headed for the kitchen, looking for aspirin.

'No, I don't think so,' said Robert. 'Wouldn't it have come up in hospital?'

Ally's seizure slowed to the occasional twitch of contracting muscles, releasing the last bit of lactic acid into her blood-stream. Robert took the spoon from her mouth and, still unconscious, she vomited. He held her until she was done. 'She's burning up,' he said. He held her for a time until Amber returned.

'I will run a bath,' said Amber. She ran the bath. Robert carried Ally through to the bathroom. He held her in his lap, and Amber helped to undress her before leaving them alone.

He wiped away the vomit in her hair and kissed her burning forehead. Standing up he carried her to the bath and climbed in fully clothed. Supporting her on his lap, he washed her clean.

'Everything all right?' Woods asked as Amber returned to the living room and began rolling up the stained rug.

'No, everything is not all right, Woods.'

She carried the rug outside to the carport and discarded it with the rubbish. Turning to enter the house, she bumped into Woods, who pulled her into his arms. She hiccupped and, for a few minutes, she let herself cry in his arms.

Woods smoothed her hair. 'I am not going to let anything happen to you. We will all get out of this safely, and when we are, I will be taking you out for dinner.'

'What about Robert's rug, are you going to fix that too?' She smiled, feeling better at the comfort of him.

Turning on the ABC radio, Woods learnt that the fire was well past them. The wind had changed direction and sent the fire away from Betty's Beach and away from Albany. The fire danger had passed them. Woods had restarted the generator, so the air-conditioning was back on.

Ally awoke in darkness. Robert was sleeping by her side, holding her hand. She was wearing his t-shirt. Her head pounded hard and her mouth hurt. In the dim light she saw the spoon on the side drawers.

'Ally, are you awake?' Robert woke as she shifted. He wrapped his arms around her, pulling her close, and shed a tear of relief.

ALLISON

'Robert, what happened?'

'You had a seizure. We are waiting for transport to get here to take you to the hospital. We don't know what is wrong. Ally, have you ever had seizures before?'

'Yes, when I was a kid, after my father left. It was stress related. I grew out of it by the time I was twelve. They told me that they shouldn't bother me again. Call off the ambulance, get the mobile mechanic out here, and let's go away. Please.'

'I think we still need to get you checked out, and I don't think we can go home just yet, let's not forget why we are here. I will get you something for that headache.' He kissed her forehead and climbed out of bed.

'Robert,' said Woods from the settee in the lounge room, 'How is Ally?'

'She is awake. It turns out that she had seizures as a child, probably because of all the stress.'

'We have a car coming in the morning so we can take her to the hospital. It may still be dangerous out here,' said Woods.

Ally walked into the room. 'Do you really think Scott Clarke is out there? Maybe he didn't survive the fire?'

'All of our cars have been sabotaged, so he was here. There is a chance that he hid down on the beach before the fire swept through,' said Amber.

In the morning, a young local constable collected them. The road back to Albany was littered with fire debris. Ally saw a charred commodore and felled, blackened trees littering the burnt bush. Gone was the lush greenery Ally had admired when they arrived. She fell asleep on Robert's shoulder and he held her close, breathing her in. Woods and Amber sat behind them in the seven-seater, their hands just touching.

Chapter Twenty-One

Children filled the seats of the hospital waiting room, with only the occasional worried parent or guardian at their side. A small girl with a mass of dark, curly hair sat nursing a splinted arm waited patiently to see a doctor. Ally caught her eye and smiled sympathetically before walking over and crouching down to talk to her, while Robert talked to the triage nurse.

'What happened to you?' she asked.

'The school bus crashed, my mummy is at work, and my arm hurts,' the girl said.

'What is your name?'

'Allison.'

'Mine too! But my friends call me Ally. It is nice to meet you.' Ally held out her hand, and the girl shook it gently with her good hand.

'Are you a doctor?'

'No, but I could sit with you for a while. Wait here a minute.'

'Robert, I don't belong here,' said Ally, walking towards him. 'These children need help, not me.'

Turning to the nurse, she continued, 'Is there anything I can do to help?'

Robert saw the determined look she wore and told the nurse, 'I am a trained rescue trauma medic with the Australian Air Force. Ally is kind, caring, compassionate and capable of anything.'

'Maybe I could just comfort the children while they wait for their parents?' said Ally.

'We could help too,' said Amber, appearing with Woods at her side.

'Great, the fire has left us short staffed. Our canteen has turned into an overflow waiting room, and there are only two doctors here. We are trying to get help from surrounding towns, but it will take time.'

'Okay, where do you want us?' asked Robert.

'The kids in the blue chairs need their details taken: name, date of birth, address, parents' whereabouts, and where it hurts.'

'That sounds like a job for me,' said Ally.

'Do you think you can take temperatures too? Just let me know if any temp is over thirty-nine degrees,' she said, passing over a thermometer and clipboard.

'Sure,' said Ally, turning on her heel and getting to work.

'I can start contacting the parents, unless you already have someone doing that?' asked Amber.

'That would be great. We have no one to spare, and there is a growing list of names and numbers on the triage fallout screen over there.' The nurse pointed to the desk on the far left of triage.

'Okay, I am on to it,' she said to the nurse.

'Medic?' the nurse asked, turning to Robert.

'At your service, ma'am!' He held his hand to his forehead in salute.

The nurse smiled tiredly. 'Head into the emergency department, gown up, and I will start shuttling in the minor cases for you to assess. Some might be okay to go home, but if you are unsure put them on the doctor's list.' She pointed down the corridor and indicated for Robert to go.

Finally, it was Woods's turn. 'I would like to help, and I will, but first one of the children told me that the bus driver swerved to avoid hitting a man who was running across the road. I am Detective Woods, and the woman making the calls is my partner. This man could be the same man that we are investigating. He's very dangerous, and I need to find him. I need to speak to the bus driver.'

'I am sorry, detective, but the driver wasn't brought in through here. Hang on, I will see if I can find out where they did take him.'

A quick call revealed that the driver had been taken directly to surgery.

'He is in recovery, room thirty-four, detective.'

'Thank you,' said Woods. 'I will come back to help as soon as I can.'

'I am on the tail end of a double shift that doesn't look like it's ending anytime soon. I could use some coffee.' She smiled and called the next patient into the examination rooms.

Woods stopped by Amber's desk and waited as she finished her call. 'You okay?' he asked.

'I will never get used to telling parents bad news about their kids. Even when it is not a fatality, it is still shit. There is that brief moment after I introduce myself, that I can hear them holding their breath, waiting,' said Amber.

'You are doing a great job, and I don't envy your task. How many to go?'

'There are at least fifty here and apparently there are more in the canteen, so I will just have to keep working through it until it is done,' said Amber.

'I would love to help you, but I have a lead. The bus ran off the road because the driver swerved to miss a man running out of the bush. He wasn't found at the scene. I will talk to the driver now and see if we can get a positive identification. Don't let Ally out of your sight.' He kissed her cheek and squeezed her hand before leaving her.

'Like I said, I wouldn't be upset if he brought me back that coffee,' called the nurse after Woods as he headed down the corridor.

An hour later, Amber found Woods in the coffee room.

'Was it a positive identification?'

'Yes, I am afraid so.' He handed her a cup of coffee from the tray of cups he had prepared.

'Well, I may have some good news. State Emergency Services have found a man at Crows Point, a few kilometres up the road from the accident. It looks like he fell. He is still alive, but they said he is falling in and out of consciousness. We have him, I'm sure of it. State emergency services are out there now and are bringing him here.' She sipped the coffee and smiled.

Woods watched her take another mouthful before she continued. 'I thought you might want to notify the local police, get them to make a positive identification at the scene and put the bastard under arrest.'

Woods nodded. 'Good work. How is it going in here?'

'All right. I would like to stay and help for as long as I am needed if that is okay.'

'Sure, I don't see why not, as long as you feel up to it. It has been a hell of a weekend. Some parts were brilliant, definitely the best birthday ever, but I am exhausted.' He smiled at her.

She returned the smile. 'I enjoyed it too. We still on for dinner?'

'Definitely,' he said, a sexy smile lighting up his face. 'But, for now we have work to do.' Amber nodded in agreement.

'How is Ally holding up? We should think about getting her on the plane to Perth. She still needs medical attention, and it wouldn't do her any favours to run into the bastard,' said Woods.

'I will get onto the airport and see what I can organise. She seems okay for now. I've been checking in with her, so has Robert.'

At Crows Point the rescue was halted as the message came by radio that their victim was allegedly wanted on murder and a string of other charges.

'What a real piece of work,' said Officer Charlie.

'Are we sure it is him? Maybe we should just leave him to the crows?' said Grace, a volunteer State Emergency Services veteran.

'Well, he fits the description perfectly,' said the officer. 'Hello, Scott Clarke, how are you doing down there? Can you move?' he yelled over the crag.

Lying amongst the jagged rocks and charred undergrowth, Clarke raised his head to see who was shouting down to him.

'No, my leg is stuck,' he replied.

The rescuer prepared to abseil down the crag with a backboard and first aid supplies.

ALLISON

'Grace, you are not going,' said Charlie, seeing her gear up.

'But it is my roster, my turn to be on the ground,' she protested.

'I am not letting you go down there alone. He could be armed for all we know.'

'Well, shoot the bastard in the head first. Then I will retrieve the body,' she said.

'Grace, get your gear off. You are on ground support, and that is an order,' said the captain.

'A little fresh aren't we, captain? You could at least offer to buy me some dinner first.' She laughed at the blush in his cheeks. She was old enough to be his mother, and she loved to wind him up.

Turning to the other rescuer on site, 'John, go down and get him geared up ready for retrieval.'

'Um, I would rather not, captain, if Grace says that she can handle this then she can, and I won't be standing in her way,' said John.

'Okay, Grace, you win. When you can, slip him this.' He handed over a hypodermic sedative. 'Do it as soon as you have taken his vitals. He could be armed. Can you sail with a vest on?'

'Seriously, cap, the guy can't sit up. Do you really think it is necessary?'

'Yes, I do.' The captain held out the syringe.

'Is it legal?' Grace asked.

'Yes, I believe that this patient is a danger to an SES Officer and to himself. Now get to work, my wife will have dinner on the table in an hour. It has been a bloody long day and I want to go home.'

'Yes sir!' she said laughing, before jumping off the crag.

Ally was adamant. 'I don't care. Restrain him and arrest him, but I am not leaving while I can still be useful here. That prick has had far too much control over my life already. It stops here.'

'Ally, I don't like it. For starters, you need medical attention yourself.'

'I'm in hospital, Robert. If anything happens, I am sure someone can help me.' Her eyes were tearing up, 'I am so tired of feeling useless, of needing to be taken care of.'

'Come here, Ally,' said Robert, taking her into his arms while a few of the older kids whistled.

They kissed modestly and smiled. 'It is nearly over, Ally. Soon we can start our own life together wherever you want.'

'I am sorry you had to go through all of this.' Ally rested her head on his chest.

'Never apologise to me. This was not your doing. I would walk through hell for eternity for what we have. I would do anything for you.'

Ally pulled away slightly. 'Maybe he will die from his injuries? And then we would never have to worry again. God, what an awful thing to think, I can't let him make me into a monster too.'

'We should get back to work,' said Robert, kissing her softly and reluctantly pulling away.

Scott Clarke was unconscious when he arrived at the hospital. A police guard was stationed outside his private room in the hospice wing.

The doctor arrived just as Clarke was coming to. 'Where am I?' He pulled his arms against the restraints. 'Albany Hospital, sir, it seems you've had a fall,' replied the young doctor.

ALLISON

'Why am I wearing handcuffs?'

'Because you are under arrest,' replied the officer on guard.

'I need to examine the patient,' interrupted the doctor. 'Can you wait outside, please?'

'Call me when you are done,' said the guard, exiting the room.

'Before you leave, can you please undo Mr Clarke's cuffs? I cannot examine his back injuries while he is cuffed to the bed,' said the doctor.

The officer raised an eyebrow. 'Doctor, are you aware of who this is? He has been positively identified for a string of violent crimes across the state.'

'What crimes?' Clarke interrupted. 'I was on a holiday with my family. Where are my wife and son?'

'Give over,' said the officer. 'We know who you are. You are Scott Clarke, a murderer and rapist. A filthy scumbag who is going down.'

'I do not understand what you are talking about. Where are my wife and son? We swerved to miss a kangaroo on the road. I went to get help!' Clarke screamed. His heart monitor was racing.

'Officer, you had better find out if there is a mistake. If he is telling the truth, there could be others injured on the highway.'

'Please, help them!' shouted Clarke.

'I will check with the detective,' said the officer, unlocking Clarke's cuffs and leaving them alone.

'You believe me, don't you, doctor, I never did those things, I couldn't. Never!'

'Yes, it is all a big misunderstanding. We will get this all sorted out, and they will find your family. Try to relax. I need to examine you,' soothed the doctor.

'This is embarrassing, may I use the toilet first,' said Clarke.

'Yes, of course.' The doctor gestured to the bathroom before turning his attention to the patient's file.

Behind him, Clarke took the doctor's stethoscope from the bedside table and, in one swift move, lowered the cord over the doctor's head and pulled tight around his throat. Clarke dragged the doctor into the ensuite and smashed his head into the sink, breaking his skull and leaving him in a pool of his own blood. Scott Clarke then climbed out of the ground floor hospital window in his open-backed hospital gown.

Chapter Twenty-Two

Woods and Amber followed the policeman back to the room where they found the doctor in the ensuite clinging to life.

Woods looked at the young officer. 'What were you thinking? I should have been called the moment he woke up.'

'Ally!' said Amber.

'She is in the garden with a few of the kids.'

Amber ran through the corridors and out into the grounds, but Ally was gone.

'Where is our backup?' Woods shouted. 'Get those kids inside, officer, and get us back up! We will search the car park; you and your costumed friends search everywhere else!' Woods ordered.

The car park was open planned; gridded, and it was easy to take in. There were twelve cars in the lot, no people, and no movement.

'If he has got her into a car...' Amber's voice trailed off. 'Let's get a look at the tape from those security cameras,' said Woods.

In the empty security office, they found the current tape still recording. It only took a few minutes to see that Clarke had Ally. They watched as he forced her into a white Toyota Land Cruiser.

'Looks like he is headed towards Albany Highway,' said Amber.

'Get Robert and tell the costumes where we are headed, then meet me at the front. I will get the keys for that State Emergency Services Cruiser over there. It will be the only way we can keep up with him if he goes into the bush.'

Scott had bound her hands with electrical tape he had found in the glove compartment of the stolen car. He drove with his naked arse on the seat and blood stains encrusted on his arms. His expression was wild.

'Cat got your tongue?' he asked. Ally didn't answer.

'I bet I can help you find it, make you use it, make you scream. Do you know all the trouble I had to go to because of you? It is because of you that I had to kill Renee and David.' He searched her face, eyes flicking back and forth between her and the road.

Ally focused on a small, plastic toy the type kids get from a Kinder Surprise. It looked like a hound, maybe a puppy.

'Why are you doing this?' she asked between her teeth.

'Because, Allison, you think that you are too good for me, you think that you are special. I had to show you that you are nothing but a fucking whore. I needed to take you down a peg or two, show you what a powerless stuck-up bitch you are.'

'I never did anything to you.'

Clarke laughed. 'I want to kill you, but first I will hurt you, and if that flyboy boyfriend of yours follows us I will make him watch me fuck you. Your mouth, your cunt, your arse. Then I

ALLISON

will fuck him in front of you and then you will watch each other die slowly, so slowly. Then I will be free from Allison. Free to move on to my next kill.'

The pressure in Ally's head rose. Her heartbeat was thumping in her ears. She could deal with Scott hurting her, but Robert- she could not bear the thought of something happening to him, the first true love of her life. She battled to stay calm. She had no way of knowing what he would do if she panicked. She saw a police roadblock in the distance on the road heading south as they turned north. His laughter pierced the sound of the blood drumming in her ears, and she was gone. A fit took hold of her.

Somewhere in the distance, in a place of consciousness, she heard dark laughter. Ally's body shook violently. Without a seatbelt to hold her in place, her head bashed against the dashboard of the cruiser, leaving a cut above her eye. Drooling. Ally fought for control of her own body.

Scott Clarke stopped the car.

'Oh no you don't! You will not rob me of the pleasure of killing you.' He folded up her shuddering body and threw her into the back seat. Leaning across her he restrained her with the seatbelts, and he turned her onto her side. He stood back to watch her. Scott began touching himself. 'I should jump on now, fuck you. At least you won't be a dead root.'

Losing control of her bladder saved Ally from indignation. 'Filthy bitch,' said Scott Clarke, climbing back into the driver's seat.

A few kilometres down the road, Scott turned sharply onto a bush track. The restraints bruised Ally, but they stopped her from hitting the floor. Her body calmed, and she slipped into unconsciousness.

Twenty minutes farther down the track, which was lined with scrub and tall karri trees, a clearing opened up. In the middle were two empty sea containers and planting equipment, an abandoned forestry project that had been deserted when the government had changed hands and the policy was forgotten.

Ally awoke on an old, steel-frame bed. The mattress stank of piss and mould. She was naked and stretched out like a starfish, hands and legs bound to the bed frame. The walls of the container were made of bevelled steel; there were no windows. Light shone into her prison through a hole in the doors. Pulling and twisting, she tried to free herself from the restraints.

Dried blood caked the creases of her eyes and mouth. Her hair was soddened. Mosquitoes buzzed and tormented her skin.

Her muscles were weakened from the fit. She wanted this to be over. If Scott killed her now, Robert would be safe.

'Help!' she yelled, trying to draw him out. Her voice cracked, but she tried again. 'Help me, help me!' she cried. A wide tunnel of light spread across her as Scott opened the door.

'That won't do you any good out here, Allison.' He laid down an old vegetable crate where she could see it. 'Look at what I have here for you,' he sneered. 'How do you think this will feel inside of you Allison?' Clarke showed her the jagged ends of a rusty seed planter. 'Or this perhaps? Do not worry, I have loads of things in here for us to play with. But we will have to wait until your boyfriend finds us. I know he is looking for you. That wanker is always looking for you. I know because I was looking for you too.' He held her cheeks between his thumb and forefinger. 'You are a filthy bitch, Allison.' He licked the blood on her face. 'I am going to have to wash you up. I want you to look nice for the party.'

ALLISON

He left her, and Ally willed herself not to cry. There was nothing she could do now except die.

A spurt of water hit her from the door, thick and hard. Scott assaulted her with an emergency fire hose, spraying her face and arms, legs and breasts with cold dam water. It bruised her flesh. Ally felt the electrical impulses in her body changing. She felt it building and again she was gone. Her body shook violently.

Scott stopped the flow of water and threw the hose out of the sea container. He watched her. The hospital gown tented where he hardened. This time he took hold of it and wanked himself furiously as he watched Ally fight with her own body to stay alive.

Ally's limp body lay on the wet mattress, puddled in dam water and piss. Scott shot his load onto her torso, staining her. Then he collapsed onto the floor laughing. Water dripped from the surrounding walls. 'This will never do,' he said to no one. Then he got up and left her alone.

'We must have passed them,' said Robert. His heart racing, panicked.

'Amber, call in again, check the chopper,' said Woods, driving around the weekend traffic.

'Great, why weren't we told?' She hung up the phone. 'Fucking idiots. A white land cruiser has been seen outside at an old, abandoned reforestation project depot off Albany highway, just before Willhouse Junction. Before the barricades.'

Woods spun the car around, barely missing oncoming traffic, and headed back towards town.

'Robert, we will find her,' said Woods. Amber reached forward to touch his shoulder from the back seat.

Robert nodded his head and prayed silently that they would not be too late. He couldn't live if anything happened to Ally. He loved her so much. He had to be with her now, and when he found her, after he had killed that bastard, he resolved that he would never let her out of his sight again.

'Look, there's the turn off!' Amber shouted.

A sharp turn sent Amber hurtling across her seat towards the door.

'Seatbelt!' Woods scolded.

Following Clarke's tracks through the bush, they stopped at the clearing. Wood slowed the car. 'Call for that back up now, we can't let this mongrel get away.'

They approached the clearing, stopped the car and inched their way toward the sea containers. The first one was loaded with fertiliser and planting tools, the second was where they found the bed. The walls and roof were dripping water; the cut-off ties of Ally's restraints were dangling from the bed frame. Amber found Ally's clothes crumpled on the floor and she gestured the discovery to Woods, who said nothing.

'Let's get out of here,' said Amber. 'I will call in for tracker dogs. You two look around outside. They can't be far away.'

As Woods and Robert headed towards the door, it slammed shut. They raced for the exit and Amber pushed on the door. It opened.

'Just the wind,' breathed Woods.

'Do you think she is still alive?' Robert's voice broke as he asked.

'Yes, he isn't the type to conceal a body. He is too cocky for that,' said Woods.

ALLISON

'Look! Tyre tracks, leading that way,' said Amber. 'Let's go get this bastard.'

The trio pile back into the car. 'Contact control and tell them to get that fucking eye into the sky!' said Woods.

'I already did boss. They are on the way. It's going to be fine.' She caught Wood's eye in the rear-view mirror. 'Fine,' she repeated.

When Ally woke her limbs were lead-heavy, her mouth tasted of iron. She opened her eyes and looked down.

Scott had dressed her in a satin red evening dress, like the one she had left in storage. Or maybe it was hers? It fitted. Ally's hair was wet and smelt of Pantene, and for a moment she thought it was over and she was safe. She looked up, almost expecting to see Robert.

Across a candle-lit dinner table sat Scott Clarke, wearing a white shirt, holding out a glass of champagne and smiling. 'Welcome back, Allison.'

She took the glass and inspected her surroundings. It looked like they were in a hotel. *Someone must have seen him bring her in here. I could get help. My hands are untied.*

'It is going to take a while for your boyfriend to catch up and I thought you might be hungry. You sure needed a clean up, so I brought you here to my new gig. When I followed you down to Albany, I came across a want ad outside this place. I am the new caretaker, so I closed it down last week to take care of it. Don't get any ideas, no one will hear you scream here.'

Ally felt her ankles taped to the legs of the chair. 'You bastard, why are you doing this to me?'

'Well Allison, I could say it was because I had a terrible childhood; my father was an alcoholic, my mother a whore. He used to beat me, so did my brother. My mother was a lunatic, my dad was a drug dealer. It was the drugs, it is the voices, it was this or maybe that. But Allison, the truth is that since the first time I did it to you, I enjoyed it. The first time I sliced a knife along a homeless guy's throat, I really liked it. I came right there as he bled into my hands. You are not the source of my pleasure Allison, how narcissistic of you to think so. Many things get me hard.'

'You are mad!' she said.

'Yes, now drink up and relax I don't want to have to clean up your piss again. This is a genuine Berger carpet you know, and piss stinks. I promise that there is nothing in your glass but pure champagne. Are you hungry Allison?'

Ally was ravenous. On the table was a tray of chicken and prawns on a bed of lettuce, avocado, tomatoes and olives. Alongside the tray was fresh bread and strawberries. She shook her head no.

'Eat! I want you to be fit and healthy, we could be here awhile. Eat!'

She took a piece of bread from the table and resisting the urge to gorge, she chewed slowly, wincing as she swallowed.

She watched him eating voraciously. His mouth open, lips smacking, chicken grease around his mouth and fingers. How he had changed. It was hard to imagine that she had once thought of him as kind and sensitive.

'Here.' He shoved a piece of chicken in her face. 'Eat!'

She took it and despite her vegetarianism, Ally ate as ordered. Then she drank the champagne in small sips. She didn't want the alcohol to affect her, but she was so thirsty.

'Can I please have a drink of water Scott?' she asked quietly, trying not to sound needy.

ALLISON

He looked across the table at her as if she had spoken another language.

'Scott, may I please have a glass of water,' she asked again, more confidently.

He got up and fetched her a bottle of water from the minibar fridge. 'We used to be friends, didn't we Allison songbird?'

'Yes.'

'Then you had to go off with that cunt just because I fucked that blonde at that party. I couldn't help it, the bitch needed it.' He sneered at the memory of it, feeling himself harden. 'Are you horny Allison, thinking about me inside of you?'

She looked at him. *I would happily die now rather than think of you inside me, you fuck!*

'Too horny to talk, are you? Bet you are all wet down there. Well my dearest Allison, you are going to have to wait, but I promise you that our next fuck is going to be a ripper! I brought all those toys I found at the plantation depot with us. I didn't forget a thing. Eat up.'

'Where are they?' asked Robert, his voice louder than he intended.

'Amber,' said Woods.

'There have been no sightings of the car anywhere on the highway. She was on the phone to the local police. 'Hang on, a couple had their car high-jacked by a guy in a hospital gown from a picnic spot just 10 kilometres this side of Williams. Seems he has dumped the cruiser.'

'We are almost there,' said Woods.

Amber placed an alert on a red Holden Commodore with the license plates 'Cheeky'.

'Woods! Clarke has been identified as the new caretaker for the Williams Motel. There is a good chance he has taken Ally there. Step on it,' said Amber.

He had untied her ankles, moved her to the bed and was spooning in a vice-like grip. 'I only ever wanted to be nice to you Allison, but you kept ignoring me, pretending like I was not there, when I followed you I know that you knew that I was there, yet you said nothing. Now you will be eternally remembered as mine, my victim. No one will remember what you did with your life, only what I did to you before I ended it. Don't try to move. There is nowhere for you to run. We need a little rest, that's all. Scotty has been a very, very busy boy.'

Her skin crawled. She could feel his erection pushing into her back. She refused to let herself cry. Stay strong, she told herself. Robert will be here soon. Ally's mind shifted, she was no longer afraid for Robert, Scott Clarke had no plan other than to out man Robert, but he was not capable of outmanning Robert. Even without a weapon, without the police, Robert was the better man. Scott's grip made it hard for her to breathe. She needed to urinate, but she couldn't move. If he slept, she was safe. For now. His hand shifted to her breast.

'There it is!' Robert pointed to the sign, flashing 'No Vacancies!'

As they pulled into the drive, the tyres on the land cruiser burst loudly. A tyre trap covered the entrance. The car swerved and tipped slightly, but Woods struggled to control it, skidding the four-wheel-drive to a clumsy stop.

ALLISON

'That was Clarke's early warning system. We need to move fast, here don't make me regret this,' Woods handed Robert a handgun. 'If you have no choice, you shoot him.'

'Thanks.'

The three approach the units. There are ten prefabricated units standing side by side, designed for the odd visitor to Williams. They listened at the door to unit 1A before Amber picked the lock. The trio search the room. Empty.

In the next unit, a stench of death oozed from an outline on the bed of two bodies. Robert looked at Woods, who shook his head. It was not Ally.

Amber lifted a corner of the blanket, recoiled, and replaced it. 'An old couple, probably the owners.'

At the door to the third room, they heard a noise as Ally was forced into the single door cupboard. She screamed for help and they hear the unmistakable sound of flesh being struck. Robert swiftly kicked the door open, gun ready. The two detectives close behind him. Clarke stood in the middle of the room, naked and hard, his penis in hand.

'You are too late. Allison and I had our fun. Shame I had to kill her when I heard your tyres burst.'

'You are under arrest!' yelled Woods and he starts reading Clarke his rights, but Robert didn't hold back. His left hook hit Clarke in the face first. His right hook spread Clarke's nose across his face. Robert's fists are smeared with blood and cuts from breaking teeth that shatter in Scott Clarke's mouth like porcelain. Clarke's eyes are swelling slits when he falls to the floor. Robert was all over him. He slammed his fists into him over and over.

Outside, back up was pulling into the motel car park. Amber found Ally in the closet, still wearing an evening dress. She couldn't see Robert bent over Clarke but heard Woods yell 'Stop!'

'You are better than him, Robert. You don't need that bastard's blood on your conscience. Bastards like him don't survive in prison. I promise. He will get his,' said Woods.

Breathless, Robert looked up to see Ally. Forgetting about Clarke, he went to her and wrapped her in his arms.

'Jesus Christ! What happened here?' asked the local sergeant as he entered the room. 'Resisted arrest, did you? You dumb bastard. Should fucking know better, broken bones make it real hard to fight back in prison. Has this prick got any pants?'

Find more information about upcoming titles at VanessaMcKay.com

Other books in the Shades of Love Series

Bali Retreat

Join James and Amber as they head to Bali for a two-week romantic retreat that sees them entangled in the Bali underworld.

When James goes missing, Amber must pull all her resources together to find him before it is too late.

Love Heals the Heart

When Meg took a job teaching Yoga at Casuarina Prison little did she know that she would fall for one of its most notorious inmates—Scott Clarke. He says that he has changed, that the years in prison have diminished his wicked impulses, that his love for her has made him a better man.

Is it possible for love to transform a monster? This is no Beauty and the Beast fairy tale, Scott Clarke was not under a spell, he confessed to his crimes and was even proud that he could do such things to innocent people.

Is Meg in danger of losing her life? Is she so blinded by loneliness and loss that she is willing to recklessly give her heart to such a man?

Also by Vanessa McKay

Bali Retreat

Lucy

When Love Heals the Heart

The Creative Writer's Toolkit

Watch for more at www.vanessamckay.com

www.ingramcontent.com/pod-product-compliance
Ingram Content Group UK Ltd.
Pitfield, Milton Keynes, MK11 3LW, UK
UKHW061221180426
11947UKWH00026B/1958